Let Me off Easy, COWBOY

CAVANAGH COWBOYS ROMANCE - 3

VALERIE COMER

Greenwords Media

Valerie Comer Bibliography

Urban Farm Fresh Romance

0. Promise of Peppermint (ebook only)
1. Secrets of Sunbeams
2. Butterflies on Breezes
3. Memories of Mist
4. Wishes on Wildflowers
5. Flavors of Forever
6. Raindrops on Radishes
7. Dancing at Daybreak
8. Glimpses of Gossamer
9. Lavished with Lavender
10. Cadence of Cranberries
11. Joys of Juniper
12. Together in Thyme

Pot of Gold Geocaching Romance

1. Topaz Treasure
2. Ruby Radiance
3. Sapphire Sentiments
4. Amethyst Attraction

Miss Snowflake Pageant

1. More Than a Tiara
2. Other Than a Halo
3. Better Than a Crown

Farm Fresh Romance

1. Raspberries and Vinegar
2. Wild Mint Tea
3. Sweetened with Honey
4. Dandelions for Dinner
5. Plum Upside Down
6. Berry on Top

Cavanagh Cowboys Romance
(Montana Ranches Christian Romance)

1. Marry Me for Real, Cowboy'
2. Give Me Another Chance, Cowboy
3. Let Me Off Easy, Cowboy

Saddle Springs Romance
(Montana Ranches Christian Romance)

1. The Cowboy's Christmas Reunion
2. The Cowboy's Mixed-Up Matchmaker
3. The Cowboy's Romantic Dreamer
4. The Cowboy's Convenient Marriage
5. The Cowboy's Belated Discovery
6. The Cowboy's Reluctant Bride

Garden Grown Romance
(Arcadia Valley Romance)

1. Sown in Love (ebook only)
2. Sprouts of Love
3. Rooted in Love
4. Harvest of Love

Riverbend Romance Novellas

1. Secretly Yours
2. Pinky Promise
3. Sweet Serenade
4. Team Bride
5. Merry Kisses

valeriecomer.com/books

CHAPTER ONE

D on't you think?"

Nathaniel Cavanagh pulled his attention back to the woman seated across the table from him. It took him a few seconds to remember her name. Kyra. That was it. "Sorry, I missed what you said."

"We should do something special for our one-month anniversary." She smoothed her hair over her shoulder and fluttered her eyelashes.

Nathaniel's collar seemed to be cutting off his ability to breathe. "We've only gone out twice."

Kyra reached across the table and ran a red fingernail along the back of his hand. "Everything great has to start somewhere."

"I, uh…"

Why had he allowed his twin to push him into dating again? He didn't want a third date with Kyra any more than he'd wanted the first one. He wasn't looking. Not really. It had been two years since the love of his life had ghosted him, and his heart was still shattered.

Noah had said his horse-loving client Kyra Cardston seemed nice. *Thanks, bro.* Nathaniel should have known better than to take the bait. If Noah thought Kyra seemed nice, he should date her himself, not pass her off to Nathaniel.

That should have been his first clue, but no. Noah was worried about him, or so he said.

Oh, Ainsley. Why, oh, why, had she left Jewel Lake without a backward glance?

He'd racked his brain — still did — trying to think what he'd said to send her to flight. What he'd done to her... besides the obvious. She'd wanted to save sex for marriage. So had he, but one thing had led to another, and they'd both given in. It had been fully mutual, hadn't it? Yes, it had been wrong, but he hadn't forced her.

With a disgruntled sigh, Kyra pushed her chair back and tossed her napkin on the table. "Excuse me. I need to use the ladies' room." She stalked away, her hips swaying in her snug cream-colored dress.

This wasn't fair to Kyra. She obviously wanted something more in a relationship than casual dating. Nathaniel didn't even want that much.

This restaurant was one of Missoula's finest, but the steak and shrimp he'd tucked away lay heavy in his stomach. Other couples and families and groups of friends gathered around nearby tables. Everyone seemed to be having a good time except him.

How had he landed here? Not physically, but mentally? *Noah. No more interfering.*

If Nathaniel was going to get over Ainsley, he'd have to

do it his own way and in his own time. It might take years. It might never happen.

His mind slid to the little box in his sock drawer. He'd been so, so sure of Ainsley's love. He'd been within days of asking her to be his forever. There'd been no question she'd say yes.

He rubbed his fingertips over his furrowed brow. How could he have judged her so wrongly? There'd been no clue. None.

Kyra slid into her chair and eyed him speculatively as the server approached the table. "May I offer you the dessert menu?"

Nathaniel shook his head. "No, thank you. May I have the check, please?"

"Certainly, sir." The server dipped his head and gathered up the plates.

"I was thinking we might share a slice of pie." Kyra's fingers found the back of his hand again.

He pulled away. "I'm sorry. I thought you said you were full?" She'd left part of her chicken Caesar, after all.

Kyra offered him a pout. "There's always room for dessert."

No. He was done. Nathaniel pushed back his chair and rose. "I'm sorry. I'll get you a piece of pie to go, and you can enjoy it at home." Alone.

She looked up at him. "It's better warm."

"It won't have time to cool off." He dipped his chin and stared into her eyes.

The sultry look morphed into an uncertain one. "I thought we were going to the symphony."

"I've changed my mind. Although, if you prefer, I'll drop you off there if you'd like to attend without me."

"Nathaniel…" Her voice held an edge of warning.

"I'm sorry, Kyra. You and I are simply not going to work out."

"You hardly know me."

"It's not you. It's—"

"Oh, that's so old." She slapped the table with both hands as she rose then advanced to his side.

Nathaniel wasn't exceptionally tall for a man, but he was taller than most women. In her heels, Kyra might be a half inch shorter, if that.

Her eyes blazed into his from mere inches away. "What's the real problem, cowboy? A smart woman intimidates you?"

Did she have to be so loud, so brash? In his periphery, he saw faces turn toward them. He cringed, hating to be the center of attention. Maybe he should simply agree with her to make this awkward scene go away.

But he couldn't do that. She'd cut to the core of who he was, calling him *cowboy* as though it was a slur. Rebuttals raced through his mind, each discarded as quickly as it entered.

Wide-eyed, the server stopped near the hostess desk, holding what was likely their check.

Not breaking eye contact, Nathaniel extended his elbow to Kyra. "Shall we go now?"

She held out her palm. "I'll take the symphony tickets, thanks. This was supposed to be *my* night."

Like he owed her anything. He raised his eyebrows and twitched his arm closer. "Outside."

"Don't like a scene, cowboy?"

So, so true. Nathaniel vastly preferred blending in and not creating waves. Too late for that now.

"I HATE LEAVING Vivienne to babysit Bella. It feels like I'm taking advantage." Ainsley Johnson shifted in the passenger seat of her friend's car.

"Vivienne's your sister. Besides, it's not every twenty-five-year-old who'd take on her teenage sibling when their mom died. I'm sure she's grateful to you and doesn't mind watching Bella sometimes."

It felt like Ainsley leveraged that far too often, but all they had left was each other. "Mom's passing has been rough on her."

"And for you." Carey shoulder-checked and angled into the left lane. "All that after your accident. Do you remember what happened yet?"

Ainsley shook her head and sighed. "A few things here and there. It's been almost two years now, and the doctors aren't sure whether my mind will ever fill in the gaps. Hence this trip."

"Well, I'm sure glad you remembered me!"

Traffic was bumper-to-bumper as they navigated around the roundabout.

"Aw, you were my best friend in Jewel Lake when we were kids. Of course, I remember you." Even though they'd rarely seen each other since.

"Then it seems you should have clear memories of the guy who fathered Bella."

"I know, right? It's too bad you were away at college that winter, or you'd know."

Carey snorted. "Or you could have told me in one of our Facetimes instead of mysteriously keeping your secrets tight to your chest."

Why hadn't she? The familiar headache threatened to blacken Ainsley's vision at the glimpse of what she'd forgotten. There was so much panic in her mind. So much that Vivienne had done most of the driving over from Spokane as Ainsley's fears ballooned. But wasn't it time to get answers?

Mom hadn't wanted her to. "Leave well enough alone," she'd said. "There's likely a good reason you can't remember it all."

What could that good reason have been? The memories were too vague. A tall, dark, and handsome man. Probably a one-night stand, said Mom. But her mother hadn't been there. She'd been in Spokane, and Ainsley had been in Jewel Lake. At least, according to the pay stubs in her purse.

Surely Ainsley wouldn't have slept with some random man like her mother thought. Like her mother had done. Ainsley was lucky Vivienne was her only sibling, the way Mom had lived. Mom refused to answer questions about parentage and said what was good enough for Ainsley and Vivienne was good enough for little Bella.

"Ainsley, are you okay?" Carey's concerned voice came from a distance.

Black spots dotted Ainsley's vision, each a pulse of pain. She shook her head ever so slightly. Maybe she should have waited to try to find her way down memory lane, but she couldn't help wondering if the darkness would ever completely dissipate if she didn't discover the truth. Which was worse, the knowing or the not knowing? She wouldn't know the answer without more information.

"Look, we don't have to go out tonight. Just because Mom and Frank bought a restaurant doesn't mean we have to go eat there today."

Ainsley rubbed both her brows. "I'll be okay. It's just… there are so many memories, but none of them are complete. The headaches will probably get worse before they get better."

The truth will set you free.

That verse from John 8 had become her beacon since Mom's passing. Ainsley desperately needed release. Needed to fill in the gaps. The only thing that could get her there was truth, even though the path would be painful.

It was already incredibly hazardous. It seemed like it had been harrowing before she'd stepped out in front of that taxi running a red light, but she couldn't recall why. She wasn't usually preoccupied — was she? And yet, the police report clearly recorded what bystanders had said.

Ainsley had *not* looked both ways before crossing the street. She'd stepped off the curb, and *bam.*

She was lucky the trauma hadn't caused a miscarriage. Bella had been the only light in the darkness. If she'd lost that glimmer, the shadows would have claimed Ainsley, too.

How did she know that?

She knew so many things she couldn't pinpoint or reason out. Yes, she needed to find the truth. It would bring clarity.

"Ainsley?" Carey's voice held more than worry. Maybe fear.

"I'm okay. Really. Let's go get dinner. There's no need to waste your mom's gift."

"You sure? Because we could go a different night. How long are you in town?"

"I-I don't know."

"Sorry. You're welcome to stay as long as you need to. Want to."

But Carey had a one-bedroom apartment. She didn't have room for three extra people.

"I'll look for a place. Look for a job." But who would hire her with her frequent sudden headaches? Someone. God had this. If she couldn't believe that, the darkness would win for sure.

The signal light began to tick, and Ainsley pushed her melancholy thoughts aside as best she could. "That's the restaurant? It looks really nice. Upscale."

"I'm so glad Mom found Frank after she and Dad split up."

Carey's parents' divorce had happened around the time Ainsley's mom left Jewel Lake. Sometimes Ainsley wondered if Viv was Carey's half-sister, since Mom had worked for Carey's dad back then. There wasn't any evidence, though, and Vivienne didn't look at all like Carey. However, the purpose of this return to Western Montana wasn't really to uncover Vivienne's parentage. It was to uncover Bella's.

Carey pulled into the parking lot next to a shiny black pickup.

Ainsley smiled. Wasn't that a sign she was back in

ranching country? She'd probably even ridden horseback, but she wouldn't know for sure until she tried it again.

Together, they walked into the restaurant's brick and wood interior. Halfway to the other end, a gorgeous woman stood facing a man beside a small table.

The woman leaned in, her face a mask of fury. "Don't like a scene, cowboy?" And then she belted him across the face.

The man's hand came up to cover the cheek she'd slapped. The woman rammed her elbow into his side as she passed him then marched toward the door.

Carey grabbed Ainsley's arm and yanked her aside. Good thing, or the angry woman's elbow might have cleared her path between them, as well.

But Ainsley's gaze snagged on the man as he turned toward them. He was… someone she knew. The woman had called him a cowboy as though it were a dirty word, but he nicely filled a black suit and tie with a light gray shirt. Cowboys wore jeans and boots and plaid flannel shirts and brown felt cowboy hats. At least, her cowboy had.

Bella's dad was a cowboy.

Ainsley blinked as the black spots danced and grew.

This man… could he…?

But the shadows merged before she could form a complete thought.

CHAPTER TWO

His cheek still stinging, Nathaniel's gaze snapped to the women who had just entered the restaurant as one of them crumpled to the hardwood floor. His breath caught.

Ainsley?

It couldn't be. Not like this. Not after all this time.

But she sure looked like his love. Shoulder-length blond hair draped over her face as she sagged.

The other woman dug her phone out and tapped at it. Probably calling 9-1-1.

Nathaniel's long legs ate the distance between them, and he crouched at the woman's side. "Ainsley?" He swept her golden strands aside and nearly wept with relief. Definitely her. He pressed his fingers to the side of her throat. Her pulse was weak but steady.

"Nathaniel Anderson? What are you doing here? Do you know Ainsley?"

He looked up at the other woman. She looked vaguely familiar… and thought his surname was Anderson. It hadn't been for over half his life. This was all so confusing. "Do I know you?"

She rolled her eyes. "I'm your cousin. Carey Anderson? Your dad was my dad's brother?"

He wasn't sure if he'd seen her since his father's funeral. "Sorry. I didn't recognize you. It's been a while."

"It has. How do you know Ainsley?"

Nathaniel hesitated. This wasn't a conversation he wanted to have in public, not with Ainsley unconscious on the floor in front of him. "We once knew each other well. I assume you were friends?" Which begged so many questions.

"Were?" Carey glanced toward Ainsley's inert body. "We still are."

"I don't understand." And the list of things he didn't grasp seemed to be mushrooming by the instant.

The sound of sirens grew louder.

Nathaniel became aware of the staff gathered around them, of the other patrons staring their direction. Before he could shake his paralysis, a woman in uniform ordered him to make room. He stumbled to his feet and watched as two paramedics assessed Ainsley and asked Carey what had happened.

"She wasn't feeling well on the drive over. She had a TBI a couple of years ago, and it caused some permanent damage."

TBI? He didn't know the term. Permanent damage, though. Two years ago. *I wonder…* "What's a TBI?"

No one replied. They strapped Ainsley to a gurney as Carey answered their questions in jargon Nathaniel didn't understand. Was Carey a nurse or something? Then they were wheeling Ainsley away.

"Wait!" Nathaniel dodged after them.

"Sir, you haven't paid your bill."

He tried to shake off the grip on his sleeve, but the words sank in. He was no thief. "Carey, wait!" he hollered as he fished his wallet out of his pocket. He glanced at the check and flung down three fifties. "Keep the change." It was way too much — especially for a date that had gone sour so quickly — but he had other things to worry about.

The ambulance zipped out of the parking lot. Carey slid into a compact car and backed out before he could stop her.

Nathaniel surged into his truck and started it with fumbling fingers. How would he keep a small white car in sight when it looked identical to half the other cars on the streets? What hospital would they take Ainsley to?

Also, did he have Carey's phone number somewhere? He doubted it. Their fathers might have been brothers, but the families had never been close. Uncle Jason had come around a lot while Dad declined from cancer and for a while after the funeral, but that had ended when Mom married Declan Cavanagh. Nathaniel and Noah had been eleven, their brother Adam thirteen. Nathaniel hadn't thought much about his girl cousins all these years.

It was simple. With the ambulance long gone, he needed to keep Carey's car in sight. Otherwise, he'd be looking for two needles in a haystack instead of just one. There weren't that many hospitals in Missoula, but he didn't want to waste time checking emergency rooms.

They might not keep Ainsley long. She'd only fainted. Right?

He frowned and tapped the Bluetooth button. "What is TBI?"

The robotic voice replied, "A TBI is a traumatic brain injury, a disruption in the normal function of the brain that can be caused by a bump, blow, or jolt to the head, or by a penetrating head injury."

Nathaniel tightened his hands on the steering wheel and scowled at the little white car up ahead as it pulled into a left-turn lane, turn signal flashing. He glanced over his shoulder and angled his truck to follow. A horn blared, but the vehicle he'd cut off slowed enough to allow him in the lane.

He needed to be more careful. He couldn't afford to get in an accident himself. Not when he'd had Ainsley in his sights for a brief moment. He'd be right there when she woke up and get answers to the questions that had plagued him for two solid years.

Prayer. He should pray. Sometimes it was easy to trust God and leave everything in His hands. Other times, not so much. Nathaniel had done everything in his power to find Ainsley when she'd gone missing. They'd had an amazing night together — one of several that glorious week — and he'd woke up to find she'd left the ranch. Cell reception was terrible that far in the mountains, so he hadn't thought much of it until he'd tried to call her that evening, and she hadn't answered. No texts, either.

She hadn't been in church Sunday, and that's when he'd felt the uneasiness give way to concern. He'd gone to her apartment. No one answered, and he had no key to go inside. On Monday, he'd risked his stepfather's wrath by shirking his duties and driving the half hour back to Jewel Lake.

Ainsley worked in the office at Creekside Academy, the private school operated by their church. But the office administrator said Ainsley'd taken a few days off. Some sort of emergency back home.

Nathaniel had left more messages. Sent more texts, but she hadn't answered. Family emergencies could be all-encompassing, right? He knew that. By the time another week had gone by, his worry had swelled even more, but it had also been tinged with anger.

When he'd finally thought to check her social media accounts, he'd found them closed. Not just inactive, but deleted. It was like she had disappeared on purpose.

How could Ainsley have done that to him? After what they'd shared? He loved her. She'd loved him. Had he scared her by hinting that he wanted to be together forever? No. She'd been smiling. Happy. Tender.

Still, he'd somehow missed a clue. Maybe ten clues. How would he know how many? He'd been totally oblivious.

She'd once told him her mom lived in Spokane, so Nathaniel had run a search there. The list of Johnsons was unbelievably long, and they'd all been dead ends.

Ainsley had simply up and vanished as though she'd never existed.

Nathaniel wasn't going to let it happen again.

AINSLEY BECAME aware of the throbbing headache as she eased toward consciousness. She blinked to open her eyes, but the light blinded her. She winced and scrunched them shut.

What had happened? Where was she?

The all-too-familiar antiseptic smell of a hospital assaulted her, but that couldn't be right. That was in her past. After her accident. Again, with childbirth.

She had a baby. "Where's Bella?" she whispered.

"Ainsley! Are you okay? Bella's safe. She's at my place with Vivienne, remember?"

That sounded vaguely correct. She'd been with Carey in Missoula. They'd been headed to Carey's parents' restaurant for dinner, where they were going to come up with a plan for finding Bella's dad. This was a sensitive subject for Vivienne, who also didn't know her father. *Join the club, sister.* Ainsley didn't know who hers was, either. But the buck was going to stop right here. She was going to figure out Bella's parentage then move on to hers and Vivienne's. The clues would be much slimmer since so much time had passed, and Mom had refused to say, even on her deathbed.

They'd gone into the restaurant, and that man had looked at Ainsley strangely. Like he knew her. Then the world had gone black.

Talk about timing.

This sounded like a hospital with doctors being paged and squeaky shoes and the rattle of curtains. "She's regained consciousness?"

"Briefly," confirmed Carey. "But she had a TBI a couple of years ago, and I know she gets excruciating headaches. I think the lights in here are too bright, because she scrunched her eyes shut again the second she tried to open them."

"It *is* bright," the other voice responded. "But it will get worse, because I have to check her pupils. Is it possible she's also dehydrated?"

Ask me. I'm here.

"I'm not sure. Sorry. We'd just entered the restaurant to be seated for dinner."

"Open your eyes if you can hear me, hon." Someone patted her arm.

Ainsley covered her eyes then opened them, trying to adjust to the brightness. The blackness had dissipated some.

By the time the doctor had checked her pupils, the spots had moved back in. "I'd like to keep her for observation, but I think it was just an unfortunate occurrence. She shouldn't be alone, though."

"She's staying with me. I'll keep an eye on her and bring her back if it seems necessary."

"Sounds good then." Another pat on Ainsley's arm. "I'm sorry about the TBI. They can sure mess life up. My sister had one."

"Thanks," whispered Ainsley. She couldn't imagine Carey and Vivienne managing Bella if she were stuck in the hospital. She needed to go home, not that she had one.

Why wouldn't God take away these horrible headaches? Why wouldn't He restore her memories? She needed to find Bella's father so her toddler would have someone to care for her when Ainsley couldn't.

It wasn't Vivienne's job. Viv would be off to college in just over a year. She'd agreed to spend the summer in

Montana with Ainsley, but insisted on finishing high school in Spokane, even if she had to live with a friend. That seemed fair enough. It gave Ainsley the summer to figure things out for her and Bella.

"Can you sit up?" Carey asked. "I'll get a wheelchair."

The thought of moving seemed painful, but Ainsley managed a slight nod. "Yes."

She heard Carey leave, but it took longer for her to return than Ainsley expected. No point sitting up too far in advance.

"No! You can't come back here."

"I need to see her."

"Nathaniel, no."

The male voice grew louder. Firmer. "You don't understand. I need to."

"Can't you see she's in extreme pain? This isn't a good time. I'll give her a message."

The curtain rattled, and Ainsley winced. She managed to get her eyes open and keep them that way.

A handsome face filled her vision as the man from the restaurant leaned over her, his dark eyes clouded with concern. "Ainsley, my love. I can't believe it's really you, after all this time."

She furrowed her brow as she stared back. He seemed familiar, but to call her *my love*? Could he be the one she was searching for? Had God truly answered her prayers in such a happenstance way? "Who are you?" she rasped out.

The man winced, his eyes shuttering for a few seconds before looking at her again. "I'm Nathaniel. Your... boyfriend."

"That TBI I told you about?" Carey interrupted. "She lost her memories."

The man — Nathaniel — turned to look at Carey. "Then how does she know you?"

"We were friends as kids. But things that happened just around the time of her accident are gone."

"Ainsley, I've been looking everywhere for you for two years."

"I've been trying to remember for two years," she rasped out. The word *trying* was still key, though. Familiarity wasn't the same thing as memory.

"I don't want to lose you again. Let me take you to the ranch. Take you home."

Was home on a ranch? She didn't think so. But a log cabin. Horses. Big black trucks like the one at the restaurant... maybe?

"She's staying with me," Carey cut in. "Until she's able to make that kind of decision for herself."

"But I—"

"Ainsley, hon. You need to think of Vivienne and Bella. There's no need to do anything hasty."

The man frowned. Opened his mouth to say something. Closed it again.

"Give me your number," Ainsley whispered. "We'll talk when I get things cleared up a little."

Nathaniel turned to Carey. "I need your number, too. I'm not letting this go. Ainsley is far too important for me to lose again."

Was this bossy man the father of her daughter?

Would that be such a terrible thing?

CHAPTER THREE

The sun hung low on the horizon when Nathaniel pulled up in front of his small log cabin on Rockstead Ranch. He stripped out of his suit and into more comfortable clothing then strode down to the corral.

Kingpin whinnied and trotted over.

"Come on, boy." Nathaniel grabbed his saddle and swung it over the gelding's back. He'd just tightened the cinch when someone spoke.

"How was the date?"

Nathaniel glanced at his twin. "You're never setting me up again, but you won't have to, anyway. Ainsley was there."

Noah blinked. "Wait. What? You found Ainsley?"

"Yeah." Nathaniel slipped the bit into Kingpin's mouth.

"Was she… was she with someone else?"

"Our cousin Carey."

"Carey Anderson?"

Noah sounded as confused as Nathaniel felt. "Apparently they're old friends. Who would have guessed?"

"I don't understand."

"Me, either." Nathaniel stuck his boot in the stirrup.

Noah's fingers tightened on his shoulder, preventing him from mounting. "Tell me everything you know."

"I need to ride." He needed to feel horseflesh between his knees and the wind on his face as much as he needed his next breath. As much as he needed Ainsley.

"I'm coming with you. Hold tight for two minutes, man."

Nathaniel settled in his saddle, looking toward the setting sun. "Move it."

In record time, Noah had tacked up Sequoia and rode out beside Nathaniel. "Talk to me."

"What do you know about TBIs?"

"Traumatic brain injuries?" Noah frowned. "Not much. I think they are sometimes a result of a head injury in a car accident or something."

"And can cause memory loss?"

"That sounds reasonable."

"Carey said Ainsley had one about two years ago."

"Why don't you start from the beginning? Because I'm not following. How did you meet up with them?" Noah shook his head. "I don't think I'd even recognize Carey or Laurel if I ran into them."

Laurel. That was Carey's older sister's name. She'd been closer to their age than Carey. "I didn't, but she recognized me. After I recognized Ainsley, who didn't know who I was." His heart felt like it had been split in two all over again.

"The beginning, please."

Nathaniel told his twin the tale, starting with the disastrous end to his date with Kyra and finishing with leaving the hospital ER with more questions than answers.

Noah whistled. "That would explain a lot."

Shadows had deepened on the upper ranch road while Nathaniel talked, but he wasn't really ready to return. The half-moon was high in the sky, so there was plenty of light.

"What are you going to do?"

Nathaniel shoved his Stetson higher on his head. "I don't know. What can I do? She doesn't know who I am."

"You don't think she's bluffing, do you?"

The words stabbed him from heart to gut as though he were a medieval soldier in a losing battle. Ainsley faking it? Was she that good an actor?

If so, maybe she'd been pretending to be in love two years ago. Pretending to follow the Lord. Pretending to be distraught they'd had sex when they'd agreed to wait. Had it all been a show?

No. It couldn't have been.

But looking back now? Two years of absolute silence. A professed traumatic brain injury. Childhood friends with his cousin, and he hadn't even known it. A childhood she'd neglected to reveal. Maybe she *had* been messing with his mind all this time.

It just didn't add up, though.

"Can I make a suggestion?"

His twin's question was a mere formality. Noah would say his piece no matter what. Nathaniel shrugged.

"You've got her number. You've got Carey's. That's way more than you had this morning."

"I had Ainsley's number before." Albeit a different one.

Why had she changed it if not to deflect Nathaniel's calls and texts?

"I'm not done."

Nathaniel rolled his eyes at his twin. "Spit it out already."

"So, leave it for a couple of days. And pray. Pray like you've never prayed before, and I'll do the same."

Pray like he'd never prayed before. Wasn't that what he'd done two years ago when Ainsley ghosted him? It had done no good then. Why would it help now?

"Maybe call our brothers together and tell them what's up. They'll pray, too. And Mom."

Brothers. Plural. For all that Noah spent half his time running his mobile blacksmith business away from Rockstead, he considered not only Adam but Declan's sons as brothers.

Nathaniel had to admit Blake and Ryder weren't too bad, and Travis was a whole lot less surly since he and Dakota had reunited last summer. Or maybe it was that Travis had turned into a townie. The man drove up to Rockstead every day for work, but he didn't have to put up with Declan in his off-hours anymore.

Confide in Mom? She seemed so fragile these days. Someday Nathaniel was going to confront his stepfather with how the man had treated his wife in the years of their marriage. Mom deserved better. She'd had so much love and joy from Dad and so little from Declan.

Would updating her and asking her to pray for Ainsley — again — be a good thing or not? The little energy she seemed able to muster went into homeschooling her other set of twins, Declan's and her fifteen-year-old daughters. Mostly Alexia and Emma ran wild.

No, he didn't want the whole family to know. They'd talk it to death, and he didn't know anything. He hated when people looked at him in pity.

"...give Nathaniel wisdom and patience. You know he wants Your will, Lord."

Nathaniel tuned in to his brother's prayer. Did he really want God's will, or did he just want Ainsley? He'd messed up on that one two years ago, so maybe he deserved what he'd received.

When Noah finally said amen, he turned to Nathaniel. "I just thought of something."

"Hmm?"

"Remember a while back when I thought I'd seen Ainsley in Saddle Springs but then decided I must have been mistaken, because she should have recognized me?"

Nathaniel's heart stuttered. He'd been fixated on that for weeks, but the clue had not been a clue any more than any other rumor he'd heard. That was to say, it had fizzled to nothing, and he'd finally tucked the thought away. He took a deep breath. "I remember."

"That woman I saw. Maybe it really was Ainsley. If she had a TBI, it's possible she didn't recognize me at all."

Nathaniel nodded.

"She was pregnant, Nat. Round-like-a-basketball pregnant."

CAREY PARKED on an overlook beside a small lake glistening in the afternoon sun. "So, this is Jewel Lake. Look familiar?"

Ainsley nodded. She'd been in this exact spot at least once. She scanned the town with its green square beside the beach. The stars-and-stripes flew over a domed building. Town hall, right?

From this vantage point, tree-lined streets intersected at right angles for dozens of blocks. Large brick buildings near the waterfront gave way to apartments which gave way to single-family dwellings. Beyond the downtown core, a ribbon of trees snaked away from the lake, a tall spire piercing them.

That was Creekside Fellowship, with the academy where she'd worked on the same property. She'd looked up the location when she'd found her pay stubs at the bottom of her purse.

"There's a playground by the school." Carey glanced over her shoulder at Vivienne. "We used to attend church here when I was a kid."

Vivienne snapped her gum but didn't reply.

Ainsley's heart hurt for her sister. Between them, they had so many questions and so few answers. Still, it hardly seemed fair to saddle the teen with a toddler over and over. One summer. That's what Viv had promised. At least Bella had fallen asleep in her car seat in the short drive from Missoula. Maybe she'd stay asleep and get a real nap.

"Still want to go down there?"

"Yes."

"Word of advice." Carey bit her lip as she glanced over. "Stick to the academy. The secretary at the church office is a terrible gossip. She'll spread your business faster than you can blink."

That sounded vaguely familiar. "Okay." Ainsley was in no position to argue with anyone who had her best interests at heart... or seemed to.

Carey drove through the outskirts of town then turned down Agate, where woodlands lined one side of the street and nice houses the other. The trees gave way to a grassy field beside the church, which was separated from the school by a parking lot.

Ainsley's gut twisted. Was she really ready to find the truth here? Maybe she should have called Carey's cousin instead. The cowboy had claimed to be her boyfriend. He was likely Bella's father. But what if she'd run because of abuse? He seemed so intense. That woman had slapped him, and he'd been kicked out of the hospital because he'd pushed his way into her ER cubicle.

He hadn't followed the rules. Could he be trusted?

Carey turned off the car. "Do you want me to come in with you?"

"No." Ainsley looked at her little daughter, blond curls plastered to the side of her head as she slept in the car seat. *For you, Bella.* "I've got this."

Vivienne pushed open her car door for air and pulled out her phone. Probably texting her friends back in Spokane. Viv had made a huge sacrifice for her sister and niece.

That meant Ainsley had to do her best. No hiding and letting the darkness win. She exited the car and straightened her top over her capris. There were only a couple of cars in the lot. Maybe no one was even at the school on summer break. She should have come before school let out.

She couldn't have. Not with Mom so sick and Vivienne in classes. This was the best she was going to get.

The door was unlocked, so Ainsley entered the dimly lit foyer. The desk where she'd worked — ha, she remembered! — was vacant, but a light shone from the open door beyond. Priscilla Cantrell, administrator.

Ainsley made her way to the doorway and knocked on the jamb. "Hello?"

Chair wheels squeaked. "Yes?" Then Priscilla stepped into sight, and her eyes widened in shock. "Ainsley Johnson! Is that you?"

"Hi. Yes."

"What on earth happened to you, girl? It's like you dropped off the planet."

"I-I was in a bad accident. I still don't have all my memories back."

Priscilla's eyebrows tipped up. "You sounded fine when you called to say you needed a few days off. But then — nothing."

"There was... that was... that's a piece I don't remember. According to my mom, I was back in Spokane for a few weeks before the accident."

"A few weeks. But you didn't call again to explain even that part."

"I'm sorry? I don't remember why. I know that sounds like a cop-out, but something happened that sent me away in the first place. Do you... do you have any idea what that might have been?"

"You're asking *me*?"

Ainsley nodded. But it was no use. Her former boss didn't believe her. Or if she did, she didn't know anything to help.

"Look, I've got nothing. One day you're all smiles and filling this school with sunshine, and the next, you disappeared."

"Why... why was I so happy?"

Priscilla slowly shook her head, her eyes still penetrating Ainsley's. "The students teased you that you must be in love."

She could only hope she had been, since that's when Bella had been conceived. She swallowed hard. This was so difficult. "Do you know whom I was dating?"

The administrator laughed. "You're kidding, right?" But then she looked more closely. "You're not kidding. You don't remember."

"I honestly don't."

"Wow, that stinks."

"Tell me."

"I'm sorry, but you didn't confide in me. It was like you had this big, happy secret you didn't want to spill to anyone. At any rate, you kept it close to your chest." Priscilla studied her. "Why now?"

Tell her about Bella, or not? Not this time. "My mom passed away recently, and a few memories have resurfaced. I'm trying to trace what happened. I was... afraid, I think."

"Not much to be afraid of in Jewel Lake, unless someone unsavory from your past showed up, maybe?"

I know who you are, Ainsley... Go. Don't come back.

She stared at her former boss, trying to stay grounded in the moment though the blotches swirled in her vision.

Who had said those words? A man. Nathaniel? That didn't seem right. But that conversation, such as it had been, had to do with the cowboy.

If only she could remember.

This was more than she'd had before, though. Maybe the truth would burst out of its cage any minute now.

She waited.

"Are you okay, Ainsley?"

"Not really. But I will be, I think. I just need to remember, and that's why I've come back. I have a few pieces, and being back in Jewel Lake is fitting some of them together. Maybe a complete picture will emerge."

But that male voice had threatened her. Did that man live here in Jewel Lake? Would she accidentally run into him, and he'd recognize her before she recognized him? Would the entire jigsaw puzzle snap together before he did whatever he'd threatened to do?

"Ainsley?"

She forced herself back to the moment. "If you think of anything, could you let me know? Let me give you my number."

"I've got it in the files, unless it's changed?"

"My phone was crushed in the accident. All my contacts and texts and photos, gone. My mother figured a new number was best under the circumstances."

Melody handed her a scrap of paper and a pen. "Your story is so strange it must be true. Who'd make something like this up?"

"I know, right?" Ainsley jotted her phone number down. "I could sure use some prayers."

"You've got them. And Ainsley? If there's anything you need, please let me know."

Tears surged to her eyes. "You'd give me another chance?"

"God gives us as many chances as we need."

"Thanks." And it was true. Maybe there was a reason Ainsley hadn't died in that accident. Maybe God wasn't finished with her yet.

Maybe the truth would still set her free.

CHAPTER FOUR

Nathaniel patted Kingpin's rump and sent the gelding trotting off into the corral. It had been a busy few days at Rockstead, but it was all physical labor, leaving way too much time for Nathaniel's brain to replay meeting Ainsley again from every possible angle. How long did he need to give her? Would she disappear again?

"Don't be so stupid," Alexia yelled from inside the stable.

Wow, he wasn't the only one off his game right now. He pivoted on his boot heel and entered the stable to see his twin sisters glaring at each other, both with their fists propped on their hips. "Hey, what's going on?"

Alexia narrowed her gaze at him. "None of your business."

"It's always my business." He smiled at her then Emma. "Especially when you're disturbing the horses."

Emma stuck out her tongue at Alexia then led her mare

out the open doors. "I'm not the stupid one. You are. And are you coming, or not?" She swung up onto Desiree.

"There's nothing else to do around here." Alexia scowled as she marched past Nathaniel, leading Domino. Then her face brightened into a smile. "Unless you'd like to drive us to town?"

Conniving little minx. "Not really." Although he could look up Ainsley while his sisters were at a friend's house. No, he wasn't going to help these two.

"Pretty please? With sugar and spice?"

Emma snorted. "Sugar and spice don't sway guys, Lex. And Nathaniel hates people. Why would he go to town? You want a ride, try Blake. He at least has a social life."

Ouch. But it would hurt more if it wasn't so true. "You two going for a ride? Dinner is in less than an hour."

Alexia curled her lip at him as she mounted Domino. "You think we don't know that? Dad has drilled the schedule into us since we were born. There's an airhorn for meals, and cattle prods for everything else."

He couldn't help the laugh. His stepfather was rigid, no doubt about it, but cattle prods? Seriously? He'd never seen one on the entire ranch.

"C'mon." Emma danced Desiree in place.

Alexia sighed as she kicked Domino's sides. The two girls cantered up the ranch road.

Nathaniel shaded his eyes and watched them go. Alexia and Emma ran roughshod over their father. While the man intimidated his sons and stepsons and pretty much anyone else who came in contact with him, he had little control over his daughters. It was going to take a miracle to get these two safely to adulthood, a goal their six big brothers had all pledged to.

It wasn't just their father who had little control over the girls. Mom didn't, either, but in her case, it was depression speaking. She homeschooled them — as she had the boys after her marriage to Declan — but it was summer break, and she'd withdrawn even further lately.

Maybe Noah was right. Nathaniel might not want to air his long johns in front of his brothers — especially the steps — but maybe a little bonding time with Mom would be good. He hadn't looked in on her for a while, and it wasn't likely she'd whisper her son's secrets to Declan in the wee hours.

Rather than go to Mom's rooms through the house, Nathaniel rounded the monstrous post-and-beam mansion to the garden that opened off her private suite in the walkout basement. He and Noah had rehabbed that space for her years ago when it became apparent she wasn't going to leave the ranch, even though she and her husband were barely on speaking terms.

Talk about a marriage Nathaniel never wished to emulate.

The gate squeaked when he pulled it open. He should grab some lubricant for that thing later.

"Who's there?" Mom's voice came from deep inside the luxuriant garden.

Maybe the squeak served a purpose, after all. "It's me, Nathaniel."

"I'm in the day-lilies."

He closed the gate and made his way down the stone path amid the floral fragrance.

His mother knelt beside the path, her hair pulled back under a bandana. She wore gardening gloves smudged with dirt... sort of like her face. This garden was everything to her. It was probably the only thing holding her sanity together.

Once again, Nathaniel vowed to himself that if she ever gave the slightest indication she was ready to leave Declan, his pickup would be first in line to load up her belongings and escort her away. Today didn't seem to be that day.

"How are you, son?" She settled back on her heels and studied him.

"I've been better. You?"

She smiled, but it seemed a tired smile. "I could say the same. At least there are always weeds that need pulling and bushes that need pruning."

What a strange reply. She *liked* those mundane tasks? Huh. They gave her life meaning, something a husband, five kids, and three stepsons failed to do.

Nathaniel's heart twisted for his mother once again. He remembered the love and laughter in his childhood home, before cancer stole his dad away. He'd never been able to figure out why she'd married Declan barely a year later. Even then, he'd known it wasn't for love... yet she'd allowed Declan to give her sons the Cavanagh name.

He knelt beside her and wrapped his fingers around a weed. Giving a slow pull, he unearthed it with a good portion of the root intact, the way she'd taught him. "Remember I told you about Ainsley a couple of years ago?"

Mom cast him a sidelong look. "Yes?"

"It seems she was in a bad accident that stole her memories."

"What? Oh, no. How did you find out?"

"I'd taken Kyra to dinner at that new restaurant in Missoula. That didn't end well. She, uh, belted me one before stalking out."

Mom's gloved hand rested on Nathaniel's plaid sleeve. "Are you okay?"

"Mostly injured my pride. But just then, Ainsley came in the door. She was with my cousin Carey."

"Carey? Jason's daughter?"

"Apparently. I didn't recognize her. I don't know if I've seen her since Dad's funeral. Anyway, Ainsley passed out in this little puddle on the floor, and Carey called 9-1-1, and they hauled her off to the ER."

Mom's eyes were huge. "Oh, no."

"I followed them, of course. I had to see Ainsley. To know she was okay for myself. Mom, Carey told me Ainsley had been in an accident a while back and had a TBI. She doesn't remember me. Not at all."

"Oh, Nathaniel. I can't imagine the hurt." She wrapped her arms around him.

Nathaniel turned to gather his mother close while she sniffled. Too bad guys couldn't cry, but Declan had made sure the boys knew that was a sissy thing to do. It seemed like it might be therapeutic at times, though. Times like this.

"I did get her number, but Carey seemed reluctant to give that out even when Ainsley said it was okay. She asked me to give Ainsley a bit of time." Frustration welled again. "How much time does she need? It's been two years!"

"Oh, my son."

"Carey said Ainsley only remembered her because they'd been childhood friends. Apparently she remembers *that*, but not more recent stuff." The guarded, haunted look in Ainsley's eyes tore at him.

"Yes, Ainsley's mother worked in Jason's insurance office back then." Mom's voice was strangely flat. "Brenda left town around the time your father died."

"But Ainsley had good memories of her childhood here. That's why she came back when Creekside Academy posted that office position."

Mom nodded. "But that didn't last long, did it?"

"Just a few months." A blissful few months when Nathaniel believed in happily-ever-after.

"What caused her to leave?"

"I don't know." He had his suspicions, but they weren't really something he wanted to discuss with his mother. How could he just up and tell her—

"Were you two… intimate?"

Nathaniel closed his eyes for a brief moment. So, that's how the truth would come out. "Yes," he whispered. "We'd both agreed to wait, but then, well, one thing led to another, and we didn't."

"There's something about sexual union you can't just walk away from. It bonds you to each other, whether in a good way or a bad way."

"Is that why you've stayed with Declan?" Then Nathaniel nearly clamped his hands over his ears. He did *not* want to know about this part of his mother's life. The twins were evidence the marriage had been consummated, but he really didn't want to know if Declan still came to his mother's room at night, or she to his.

"Partly." Mom sighed. "But we're not talking about my situation here. We're talking about yours. Do you think she withdrew because she was confused about her feelings for you?"

"There were hormones, for sure, but no confusion."

"And when was the brain injury?"

Nathaniel frowned. "I haven't figured that part out. It sounded like it was a bit later, but the timing is unclear. I have more questions than answers."

"God has the answers. He knows exactly what happened."

Like he needed reminding. He and Ainsley might have been acting in private, but God had been present. Grieved that His children hadn't controlled themselves but allowed their desires to overcome their sense.

"Sometimes I think Ainsley's disappearance was my punishment for my sin. I don't deserve to be happy. I had my chance and messed up."

"Son, have you asked God for forgiveness?"

"Of course, I have. Dozens of times. Hundreds."

"What does His word say about forgiveness?"

"That He gives it. But—"

"I'm not sure where you see a *but*. First John 1:9 says, 'if we confess our sins, he is faithful and just and will forgive us our sins and purify us from all unrighteousness.' Where in there do you see exceptions?"

He knew the scripture. He did. "But I was willful."

Mom laughed, but a sadder one he'd never heard. "Aren't we all?"

"I guess." Nathaniel studied her face. "Even you?"

"Oh, yes." She swallowed hard. "I, too, am reaping what I sowed."

"Tell me."

"It has no bearing."

Nathaniel touched his mother's arm. "Do you have anyone to talk to? I have Noah, though he drives me crazy. And Adam." His oldest brother had ridden pro rodeo for years and was now back on the ranch, married to Riley. "Even the steps."

"Don't worry about me."

"Those words won't stop me. You know that, right? You seem sad all the time, and that hurts us, too."

"It's my cross to bear."

"Did you hear what you just told me? That God forgives? I seem to recall verses about Him giving joy and abundant life."

Mom looked away. "Now you're schooling your mama."

"I just want you to know you deserve happiness and peace as much as anyone else."

"As much as you?" Her eyebrows arched.

Nathaniel chuckled. "Touché."

"You're young, with your whole life ahead of you. Only twenty-eight. Don't live in the shadowlands, filled with regret. Accept God's forgiveness, and go win your girl all over again. She can't remember the past? Make new memories."

"Did you hear what you just told me?" he repeated. "What's good for the gosling is good for the goose."

"But I'm married, and you're not. You're free."

Was there someone else Mom wished she'd married

after Dad's death? Nathaniel couldn't imagine it. Wait. Uncle Jason had come around an awful lot there for a bit. He and Aunt Ellen had recently divorced. But Jason hadn't been that nice a man.

"Did something happen between you and Uncle Jason?"

Mom reared away from him, her eyes wide. "Jason Anderson? Your father's brother? Not a thing. Not ever."

She'd have to be a good actor to be pulling one over on Nathaniel with that. Huh. He'd thought the same thing of Ainsley just the other day. Maybe Mom was right.

Nathaniel needed to stop looking for secret reasons Ainsley had left him and take that brain injury at face value. She was back in the area, wasn't she? She seemed to be looking for answers.

And he'd been looking for the woman who'd claimed his heart. Now he just needed to convince her — again — that he was that man for her.

CHAPTER FIVE

I think it's a bad idea to meet him alone."

Ainsley huffed out an exasperated sigh. "Carey, I'm twenty-five years old. I lived on my own for several years. I can handle myself."

Carey raised her eyebrows. "Need I remind you that was before your TBI?"

"I'm well aware, thank you. But I need to talk to him. I need to figure out if he's the one... and if I can trust him with the knowledge of Bella."

"And you don't think you can trust me to keep my mouth shut. I'm just trying to protect you."

"From your own cousin. You said yourself you don't know any bad stuff about him or his brothers."

"But his stepdad is a control freak, and his stepbrother is just as bad."

"They aren't likely to be Bella's dad."

"One can hope," Carey muttered darkly.

"See, that's what I'm talking about. You're repeating rumors, but what do you *know*?"

Carey sighed. "I remember my uncle Joe as a peace-loving guy, and Aunt Kathryn is probably nice enough, I guess. But why did she marry Declan Cavanagh?"

"That's got nothing to do with Bella and me."

"You'd think. All those guys are in their twenties — Adam might be over thirty by now — and they're still under Declan's thumb. So, I wouldn't discount the man."

"Point noted." Ainsley checked her watch. "I'm going down to the park now. He'll be here any minute."

"I still think—"

Ainsley swept out the door and shut it on her friend's pessimistic words. Nathaniel was her only real clue, and she owed it to herself to find out what he knew. And, if he was who she suspected he was, she owed it to him to tell him about their daughter.

Lord, please protect me. I'm stepping out into the terrifying unknown, trusting You. And, yes, in the park across the street from the apartment where her paranoid friend could watch from the window. Carey would definitely be doing just that.

Ainsley crossed the street at the intersection after the walk signal shone and she'd double-checked all traffic had come to a complete full stop. One TBI was plenty for a life-time. She strolled into the tree-lined park and glanced around at the assorted humanity doing life in this space, but she didn't see the man in the suit.

Chilled even in the June sunshine, she wrapped her arms around her middle as she stood in the open, glancing around. Where was he? Had he stood her up? He sure hadn't sounded like that was an option when they'd spoken on the phone.

A lone cowboy strode across the park, tall and lean in his jeans, a snap-front plaid shirt, and a brown cowboy hat.

The suited man from the restaurant morphed with the cowboy and, with a near audible click, turned into *him*. Nathaniel.

Her heart stilled as her mind sped up. Was Nathaniel the source of the threat she had such vague memories of? He couldn't be. There was nothing foreboding in his demeanor.

He stopped in front of her, dark eyes searching hers. "Ainsley?" He reached toward her then pushed his hands into his pockets.

She'd put that guardedness there. Once she'd stepped gladly into his embrace, but that was two years in the past. Things had happened. Things that needed to be dealt with. She pushed out a smile. "Nathaniel."

"You remember me?"

"Not really, but you seem familiar."

His jaw worked, and he gave a sharp nod. "Ainsley, I don't know what happened. I don't know why you left Jewel Lake. I looked everywhere for you, but no one seemed to know where you'd gone or why you'd left. Was it... me?"

Truth. "I don't know if it was you." She studied his face, longing to smooth the worry lines. "Can you think of any reason it might have been? Did we... did we fight? How long did we know each other?"

Nathaniel pointed at a nearby bench as a trio of elderly women vacated it. "Want to sit for a bit?"

"Okay." She perched on the end of the bench, hands twisting in her lap.

He sat in the middle, angled toward her, but not touching. Good. He was respecting her space. She must be giving off panic vibes by the wary look in his eyes.

"We'd been dating for several months. I went into the church office one day in early February to talk to Eli — do you remember him?"

Ainsley shook her head.

"He's the youth pastor at Creekside Fellowship and a good friend of mine. Anyway, he was running late in a meeting, and I was set to wait for him when Mrs. McDiarmid, the church secretary, asked if I'd take a few files over to the academy."

Mrs. McDiarmid. Was that the busybody Carey had warned her about? "I worked at the academy. I found some pay stubs in my purse."

"Yes, you did. I brought you the files and stood and talked to you for probably half an hour. Totally missed my appointment with Eli, but I didn't even care. I just... I thought you were beautiful and amazing, and I asked you out, and you said yes."

It sounded like a meeting out of a fairy tale. Too bad she didn't remember it.

"Our first date was on Valentine's Day. Talk about pressure! But it was fun. We talked and talked, and when I went back to Rockstead Ranch that night, I told my twin brother I'd met the girl of my dreams."

Ainsley pressed her hand to her heart. She'd been that special person to this good-looking cowboy. "And then what happened?"

"We went out every week, but you didn't come up to the ranch." He frowned as though trying to remember. "We usually came into Missoula or took a picnic up into the mountains. I think... both of us wanted to keep our relationship a secret. For me, it was my stepfather and my stepbrothers. Noah knew — he's my twin. My other brother was away on the rodeo circuit, but I didn't want my stepbrothers to tease me and make jokes about something so precious to me. I'm not sure why you didn't want anyone to know."

"I'm not sure, either." Ainsley looked into his deep eyes. "I knew my mom had left Jewel Lake when I was eight. I had good memories, but she refused to return, even for a long weekend. I was curious about the town, so when I saw the job posting, I interviewed for it. Mom was livid when she found out I was moving here."

"Did she ever tell you why?"

"Not that I recall. Just she was so nervous and secretive that I guess I didn't want to announce to the whole world that I'd lived here before." She racked her brain, sifting through fragments of memory. "This came up again after my accident."

"I wonder why."

"I'll never know. She passed away in March."

"I'm sorry. It's hard to lose a parent."

"Carey mentioned your dad died. I never knew mine, or even who he was."

"You told me that back then." Nathaniel reached for the hands in her lap but pulled back.

Somehow, Ainsley found she welcomed his touch. She had nothing to go on but instinct and his say-so, but she trusted him. She laid her hand palm up on the bench, and he twined his fingers with hers. It felt like coming home.

She focused for a long moment on the warm pressure of his palm against hers, and drew what strength she could from the contact.

Then she took a deep breath. "I have a couple of more questions."

"Ask me anything."

"Did we — were we ever intimate?"

A shadow crossed Nathaniel's face. "I'm sorry, Ainsley. I never meant to hurt you."

That didn't quite answer the question. "Yes? Or no?"

"Yes," he whispered. "Three times in that last week. Twice at your apartment and then, that last night, up at Rockstead Ranch. When you left at dawn, I never saw you again."

There was so much to unpack in all that. "I didn't want to have sex before marriage."

"I know. You told me, and I said the same." His fingers tightened around hers. "And yet, we got carried away and succumbed to the temptation. I'm so sorry I didn't honor you as I'd meant to. As God wanted me to."

"It wasn't… you didn't force me, did you?"

"Oh, my love, no." His voice broke. "It was mutual."

This was it, then. Ainsley closed her eyes and prayed for strength. "Then I think it's only fair to tell you that you're a father."

NATHANIEL STARED at Ainsley's face. Had he heard her correctly? "I have a baby?"

She shook her head. "A daughter. Bella is sixteen months old."

He jerked to his feet and jammed his hands in his pockets again. He moved off a few steps and bowed his head. He was a father? He had a daughter! But she was over a year old, and Ainsley had kept them apart.

Ainsley's here now. But, try as he might, it was hard to focus on that when he remembered the two years of silence. When he remembered his stepbrother Travis being a part of his son's life from infancy before finally winning his child's mother over last summer. Travis might have only had Toby on weekends, but he'd still been around for all the milestones.

Nathaniel had had those moments ripped from him. He hadn't even known Bella existed. *Bella.* He tasted the name.

He pivoted back to Ainsley. She still sat on the bench, hands clenched, with her brow furrowed in worry as she watched him.

"Where is she? I need to see her."

"You will." She patted the bench beside her. "I need to tell you what else I remember."

And he wanted action, but he wasn't going to get it right this minute. He dropped to the plank seat. "Tell me."

"Something happened after that night. I wish I knew what, but it scared me."

"It wasn't me, was it?" Nathaniel stared at her. "You kissed me goodbye as you were leaving. We were going to see each other again on Sunday. We were so happy."

"I went back to Spokane. I needed to talk to my mom."

"I searched Spokane and couldn't find you. Do you have any idea how many Johnsons there are?"

"She was living with Hector Sergio, so Johnson wasn't even on the lease."

Nathaniel shook his head. Didn't that figure? "Go on."

"From the pieces Mom told me, I'd been home for a few weeks when I was in an accident. I have no idea why I stepped off the curb in front of a speeding taxi, but witnesses agree that's what I did. I was hit. Someone called 9-1-1 and I was taken to the hospital with multiple injuries, including the TBI."

That still didn't explain why she'd left. It explained — maybe — why she'd stayed away for two years. "I'm sorry."

"I realized I was pregnant, but I didn't remember you. And my mom said I'd obviously run from abuse—"

"Never. I would never have hurt you. Ainsley, I loved you." He managed to get the 'd' on the end to put it in past tense, though everything in him craved to gather her close, hold her, and reassure her that his love for her was stead-fast and forever. She wasn't ready to hear it, though. She'd obviously not been ready to hear it two years ago, and they'd only been apart since then.

"After Bella was born, I began to remember some scraps of things, but Mom was concerned I'd regret pushing myself to remember more. That I'd recall things better forgotten."

"How could she say that?" That woman! And she was dead, so he couldn't even take her to task for keeping Ainsley and Bella away from him.

"She never thought it was important for my sister or me to know who our fathers were. She said it wouldn't hurt Bella not to know her dad, either."

That did it. Nathaniel surged to his feet again. "Kids

need their fathers. Mine has been gone for seventeen years, and hardly a day goes by that I don't miss him. Just as much to the point, men have the right to know their children."

He could hardly believe he had a daughter. The truth wouldn't sink in until he saw the little girl. Would she like him? Or would she be afraid of him?

It didn't matter. He'd win her over. Both of them. Mother and child. "I'm ready to meet her."

"I tucked her in bed for the night before I came down here."

Nathaniel wanted to growl. To throw things. But that would be counterproductive. The woman he'd known two years ago had trusted him implicitly, but the one in front of him was still leery. "When?"

"When do you have a morning off? Or a late afternoon — she naps from one to three, most days."

"I can take time off anytime I want to." But that wasn't completely true. Not if he didn't want to explain his absence to Declan, and he really didn't. There'd come a time to come clean with his stepfather, but that time wasn't right now. Not when Nathaniel didn't know how this would play out.

But it was already Thursday. He'd waited two years. What was three more days? "How about Sunday afternoon? Can I bring a picnic?"

"That would be nice. Is this park okay?"

Driving this far from Jewel Lake and the snoopy people who knew him sounded just fine. He stood in front of Ainsley and held out both hands to her.

She studied him for a few seconds before allowing him

to help her stand. Then he gave her a little tug, and she stepped into his arms.

Nathaniel closed his eyes and savored the feel of her pressed against the length of him. He inhaled the green-apple shampoo she favored and listened to her erratic breathing against his chest. He wanted to kiss her — wanted to claim her — but she needed time. He could give her the gift of a little more time.

He stepped back, catching both her hands again. "Sunday it is. I can't wait." And then he let her go.

How would he survive three days without her? Ainsley hadn't even shown him a photo of Bella. He nearly called her back to ask for one, but he could do three more days.

Nathaniel had a daughter. How strange and amazing was that?

CHAPTER SIX

Nathaniel set his cooler down beside the bench where he and Ainsley had sat on Thursday. He'd sworn the Rockstead cook to secrecy when he asked her to pack something for his date that included picnic food a toddler might like. Cook had given him a knowing smile and a pat on the arm for dating a single mom. He hadn't told her the toddler was his, nor had he told Noah about Bella at all. He still hadn't wrapped his head around it himself.

He looked around the small park but didn't see Ainsley. She wouldn't stand him up, would she? No. He wouldn't borrow trouble. He was a few minutes early. She'd be here.

Lord, please give me peace and wisdom. I want to do everything right this time. I want to be sensitive to You. Sensitive to Ainsley and Bella. Please restore her memories, 'cause that would make things a whole lot easier.

Not that God was particularly swayed by His children's desire for smooth pathways. Nathaniel grimaced.

Where was she? He scanned the park again but didn't

see her. Of course, maybe thirty seconds had gone by. He marched around the park bench three times, swinging his arms, then looked again.

She'd just crossed the street, pushing a stroller heaped with paraphernalia and a bag hanging from its handlebars. Plus she wore a backpack.

Wow. He had a vague memory of all the things Travis used to pack around for Toby. It had been a lot.

Nathaniel jogged to meet her. It was all he could do not to draw Ainsley into his arms and kiss her, but he managed to restrain himself. Instead, he crouched in front of the stroller and met the big blue eyes of a little blond angel. "Hey, Bella," he said softly.

Her lips quivered as she drew back from him, those stubby legs kicking the air.

He looked up at Ainsley. "I didn't mean to scare her."

"She's afraid of nearly everyone. She'll get used to you."

What kind of life was that? But it wasn't his judgment to make, since it was likely a result of Ainsley's anxiety from her amnesia.

"Okay?" He stood and reached for the backpack, but Ainsley shook her head and pushed the stroller past him toward the bench. This was crazy. He had a visceral need to care for these two... but couldn't get close enough to either of them.

Patience. Right, he'd prayed for that. He had the rest of his life.

Ainsley took a quilt from the top of the stroller and spread it on the grass then unbuckled the little girl and stood her on the quilt. "Here you go, Bella Babe."

The little one had rolls on her thighs and wore a diaper

and a frilly pink dress. Her bare feet sported the tiniest toes Nathaniel could remember ever seeing. And those wispy blond curls!

Nathaniel's heart melted into a puddle. Bella was his. His heart, soul, and will. His hands clenched at his sides as he looked at Ainsley. "She's beautiful. She looks just like you."

Pink filled Ainsley's cheeks. "Thanks. But I think she has your nose."

"This big honker? Poor kid."

Ainsley studied his face. "I don't think it's big. Y-you look pretty good yourself."

His heart swelled, but he felt the word 'patience' deep in his soul once again. "What does she like to do at the park? Swing, maybe?"

"She's terrified of it. She'll be fine right here. I brought some toys." Ainsley upended her backpack on the quilt, and Bella dove into the pile, grabbing at plastic colored rings in assorted sizes.

Nathaniel sat on the opposite edge of the quilt and watched his daughter, hyperaware of Ainsley settling across from him. He stole another look at the woman he loved. A rush of longing jolted through him, and he cleared his throat. Ainsley met his gaze. "What are your plans now?"

She shook her head and looked away. "I don't know. When I came here, I wasn't sure if I'd be successful in finding you. I didn't have much to go on."

That hurt. Nathaniel might not have Adam's bold, brash personality or Noah's quiet confidence, but he hadn't thought he was completely forgettable, either.

He held his gaze steady. "You found me. So, now what?"

"I have to do what's best for Bella."

Nathaniel dug in his jeans pocket and pulled out the little box. "What could be better for her than having her parents together and forming a family? Marry me, Ainsley?" He tilted the open box toward her.

Ainsley's hand slapped over her open mouth, and her eyes grew wide. Apprehension radiated from her body in near-palpable waves.

Right. He'd been going to practice patience. Dumb, dumb Nathaniel.

"I don't even know you."

"But I know you. I love you. You love me. We talked about the future before you disappeared. I was planning a proposal for the next weekend..." His voice trailed off as she continued to shake her head and stare at the diamond as though it were a coiled rattler.

Bella toddled closer to him and reached out to touch the gleaming gem.

"No, Bella," Ainsley rasped out.

The baby's lower lip quivered as she looked between her mom and the shiny object.

Well, Nathaniel knew when he'd been rejected. He snapped the lid shut and pushed the box back into his pocket. If there wasn't so much at stake, he'd be tempted to walk away for a little while and cool his jets. But their relationship — if they even had one at the moment — would never recover from that.

Patience. He knew he needed to exercise it, but for him, he'd never lost his love for Ainsley. Seeing her again, seeing the beautiful child they'd created together, totally over-whelmed his good sense. Why not pick up where they'd left off?

But Ainsley didn't remember, and who wanted a proposal from a near-complete stranger?

Nathaniel wasn't sure he had enough patience to win her over a second time, but the alternative didn't bear thinking about.

THE SPARKLING DIAMOND disappeared back into Nathaniel's pocket. "I'm sorry," he mumbled, not meeting her gaze.

She'd hurt him. Again. "Nathaniel, I—"

"Don't. Please don't. I'm impatient. I messed up again. It just feels like I've waited forever for you."

The anguished expression in his dark eyes nearly did her in, but with it came the black smudges on the edges of her vision. She rubbed her eyes, praying the darkness wouldn't close in.

If only she could remember. Then she'd know why she'd left in the first place. Was it something a little chat could have cleared up?

I know who you are, Ainsley... Go. Don't come back.

There had been more words, and they'd all been ominous. If she could recall who'd said them and why, it would help. But, looking back, that half-remembered threat must be why she'd abandoned Nathaniel, even though she believed him that she'd loved him. She wouldn't have slept with him otherwise. She had to trust that about herself, because the assertion that it was wrong was deeply seated. She wouldn't have thrown it over lightly.

"Ainsley, I'm sorry." His voice was gentler this time. "I'll do better. I will. Just tell me how to love you. I'll take my cue from you."

And she was giving off mixed signals, she was pretty sure. Because she instinctively responded to him as though she loved him, and yet, the wariness won. "I-I don't know."

Bella plopped onto her bottom in the middle of the quilt, and the quivering lip at being told no finally managed to turn out a respectable sob. Little drama queen. Maybe she was just like Ainsley. Wasn't it inevitable that Nathaniel would win, and she'd marry him? He wasn't wrong about what was best for Bella, and it was like Ainsley's own cells remembered Nathaniel even when her brain could not. Maybe she should just say yes and see where it took them.

Maybe she should tell him about the voice. She'd be able to tell by his reaction if he'd uttered those words, right? If only she could trust herself. If only she knew.

Nathaniel picked up one of the plastic rings and held it out to Bella, who stopped her halfhearted whimper and looked between it and him before grasping it in her pudgy little hand. She offered him a toothy smile.

He moved the little rocking tower in front of the toddler, who lined up the doughnut and shoved it on before looking at her papa expectantly.

Nathaniel didn't disappoint her. He kept reaching for ring after ring and passing them to Bella. When the tower was complete, she clapped and grinned at him.

Suspicious moisture glistened in Nathaniel's eyes,

which caused the same thing to well in Ainsley's. She'd made the right choice to come to Montana and find Bella's dad.

"I think... I think someone threatened me," she blurted out.

Nathaniel's head whipped up, and his gaze laser-focused on hers. "Who? When? What happened?"

"Before. All I know is it was a man's voice. Something about knowing who I was, and I should leave."

"Who you *were*?" A furrow formed between Nathaniel's brows. "There's something in your past?"

"I don't remember the details. I think I went home to talk to my mom."

"So, it was about her?"

Ainsley spread her hands. "I don't know. The man said more, but his words are lost."

"You never told me anything strange about your past." Nathaniel radiated honesty. "There weren't any clues that you'd been involved in anything dangerous in the past. But then..." He studied her.

"But what?" She lifted her chin. "Tell me. I need the pieces."

"I didn't know you were friends with my cousin back then. That caught me off guard the other day."

"I probably didn't know you were Carey's cousin in the first place. She lived in Jewel Lake when she was little, as did I. We were friends and became pen pals when my mom and I moved back to Spokane. Then when I came back to Jewel Lake, she was away at college." Ainsley wrung her hands together. "She said I hadn't told her about you, either."

"Maybe I didn't mean as much to you as I thought I did, if you didn't even tell your best friend." His voice sounded flat.

Ainsley shook her head. "I don't think that's it. My mother was very unhappy that I took a job in Jewel Lake. It seems like I was trying to keep a low profile. Maybe she's the one who'd done something terrible. Besides that she was pregnant with my sister when we moved away." She offered a sardonic laugh. "Must run in the family."

Nathaniel's eyebrows shot up. "You have a sister? I don't think you ever mentioned her."

"Vivienne. She's sixteen now. Mom never said who *her* dad was, either. Mom wasn't big on those revelations."

"You don't know your father."

It wasn't a question. She shook her head.

"That's… weird." Sitting cross-legged, Nathaniel plucked a stem of grass and began rolling it up.

"Yeah, I don't think it's normal."

He shook his head but didn't look at her for a long moment. "Okay, well, that stops with Bella. However we work things out between us, please don't cut me out of her life."

"I won't."

"Promise?"

That he felt the need to ask stabbed her. "Remember that I experienced what it's like to not know my father. Everyone around me had dads that came to their recitals and soccer games and school dances. Even my friends whose parents were divorced knew their dads and maybe spent summers with them. I always felt half-complete. I won't do that to Bella."

Nathaniel studied her face before he finally nodded. "Okay. We can figure out the rest of it as we go."

By that he meant between him and Ainsley. He wanted to marry her. She'd probably relent at some point, but wouldn't it be better if she actually knew she loved him back? All this vagueness was so frustrating.

"But the fact remains that someone threatened you. A man, right? And you think it's why you left Jewel Lake two years ago."

"It's the only reasonable thing I can come up with."

"Presumably you told your mom about it."

"Probably. We were close, and why else would I have gone straight to Spokane?"

"And she's dead now, so she can't shed any light."

Ainsley winced. "She refused to talk about it. Said paranoia must be part of my brain injury. I looked it up, and that's a possibility."

"But you don't think so."

"No. What I remember is firm. I just wish I remembered all of it."

"It sounds like the key to, well, everything, is figuring out who threatened you... and then why."

She should feel relief that he'd come to the same conclusion, but the fear in her gut clenched tighter.

"We spent Friday night together in my cabin at the ranch. It was the first time you'd been there." Nathaniel watched her closely. "In the morning, you kissed me and told me you loved me. And then you left the cabin. A few minutes later, I heard your car start up — you'd parked over by the corral — and drive away."

It sounded like a story that had happened to someone else, but she nodded.

"We have terrible cell reception at the ranch, so I couldn't phone you from my cabin. That evening, after getting in from trail-riding, I called from over near the stable, but you didn't answer. I texted, and you didn't answer that, either. I didn't see you again for over two years." He took a deep breath. "Is there anything in there that sounds familiar or jogs a memory?"

Ainsley picked apart his tale and pondered the parts but finally shook her head. "Nothing." Then her eyes widened at the sight of Bella in Nathaniel's lap crooning to her baby doll.

"What?" He looked down, a soft smile crossing his face. "I didn't even notice when she did that. She likes me, Ainsley. I'll never let her down."

CHAPTER SEVEN

Blake and Nathaniel, I need you in the north ranges. You'll head out day after tomorrow at dawn." Declan forked a big bite of scrambled eggs into his mouth.

Nathaniel's heart sank at his stepfather's words. It wasn't completely unexpected. Seemed Declan sent two of them out every year about this time. Wasn't it a bit early? But it had been a warmer, drier spring than usual.

Blake socked Nathaniel's shoulder. "Whaddya say, bro? I hope you're a better cook than I am."

Not that any of them had much reason to practice. Cook ably ran the ranch kitchen and sent easy-cook meals on trail rides.

Nathaniel glared at Blake. "Doesn't take much. You can burn a pot of coffee."

Blake grinned. "What can I say? I like big fires and thick brew."

"Ugh."

Declan turned to the teen twins. "It's time you two

began learning your way around the kitchen. You will help Cook prepare for your brothers' trip."

Alexia stared at her father. "That's so sexist, Dad. I say Emma and I get to ride in the back country for a week, too. We can help."

Oh, please, no. It was bad enough driving the cows and calves to the upper pasture without having to keep two flighty teenage girls safe at the same time.

Declan pursed his lips. "That's an idea."

"We don't run a princess camp," Blake warned. "No tents, just bedrolls under the stars."

Alexia raised an eyebrow in challenge. "Even when it rains?"

"Then we, uh, sleep under a big tree and hope for the best. Right, Nat?"

Why back to him? "We've done that." They'd also taken a tent at times.

Alexia looked between them. "We're tough. Right, Emma? We can ride all day and still help."

"Sure. Nathaniel and Blake can teach us all about ranching. It would be a great learning experience. You're always saying our brains get rusty on summer vacation." Emma batted her eyes.

Alexia scowled at her and Emma jerked. "Ow."

Nathaniel bit back a chuckle at the thought one had kicked the other under the table.

Declan met Mom's gaze down the length of the long table. "I'll discuss it with your mother."

No way. Nathaniel leaned forward. "Blake's right, though. We work long and hard out there. It's not for tenderfeet. The girls will be a distraction."

"You were once a newb, too." Adam chuckled. "I remember being tasked with toughening you and Noah up."

"Thanks," Nathaniel muttered.

"I said, we'll discuss it." Declan leveled Nathaniel with a hard glare. "Now, for today, Travis and Ryder are baling hay over at Running Creek. I figure you boys should be nearly done by dusk?"

Travis nodded. "Pretty close. Count on tomorrow for wrapping it up."

"Adam, you haul the bales in."

"Yes, sir." Adam leaned back, draping his arm around the back of his wife's chair. Riley smiled up at him.

Nathaniel often wondered how Adam kept so easygoing when he'd clashed with Declan over and over about the fate of Running Creek, which had belonged to their parents before Dad's death. Mom had signed it over to Declan when they married the following year, and Adam wanted it back in the worst way. He also wanted to live over there in the house they'd grown up in and raise a family with Riley. Instead, the newlyweds were stuck in one of the tiny cabins at Rockstead while Declan dithered about the future of Running Creek.

Maybe the love of a good woman had settled Adam down. He'd once been impulsive — even running off to the rodeo at eighteen — but now he seemed settled in for the long haul.

Adam had learned patience. Nathaniel was working on it. He hated every minute of the process, and here his brothers had always figured him for the easygoing one who didn't make waves.

Having Ainsley so near and yet so far caused far more than a little ripple in Nathaniel's life. His emotions verged on tsunami-sized breakers threatening to overwhelm him and everyone in their path. Even Ainsley and Bella.

He closed his eyes for a few seconds, trying to recenter himself. He couldn't trust himself, but he could trust God. *Surely* he could trust God.

"AINSLEY! WHAT BRINGS YOU BACK?" Priscilla Cantrell entered the open office from the other side.

"I know it's a lot to ask, ma'am, but I'm wondering if you have a job opening here at the academy."

The older woman studied her. "You vanished on me last time."

Ainsley forced her shoulders not to slump. "I know. I'm sorry. There were events outside of my control." Too bad she didn't know what they were. "It won't happen again."

"If the circumstances were truly outside your control, then you can't promise they won't happen again. Can you?"

"You're right. I'm sorry." Ainsley turned toward the big double doors. It had been a long shot, yet she had to start somewhere with rebuilding her life.

"It happens the secretary who replaced you just went on bedrest with a difficult twin pregnancy."

The words sounded suspiciously like hope. Ainsley looked back to Priscilla. "Maybe this is a good time to tell you I have a toddler. I'm looking for a job, a place to live, and childcare." Just the thought of all those pieces aligning sent the darkness dancing in her periphery. No giving in to it today, though. She couldn't. Wouldn't.

If her announcement surprised the academy's principal, she showed no sign. "Parenting does tend to focus us on what's most needed to survive."

"Yes'm."

"I could really use help in the office." Priscilla sighed. "The network keeps crashing as families try to access and sign up for their fall-term classes. Caleb from Digital Design has been shoring up the system, but he's also working nonstop on the Pot of Gold Treasure Hunt website upgrades. Were you here for that?"

Ainsley shook her head. "It doesn't sound familiar."

"It's an elaborate, summer-long geocaching challenge Pastor Eli started a couple of years ago. Anyway, it's turned into a big deal, and that's great, but I could really use Caleb's focus on the school right now. It doesn't help that the entire internet seems excessively slow of late."

"Fast connections are a requirement in this day and age." Ainsley might have forgotten a lot of things, but she was sure of this one.

"You can say that again. We've got some potential investors in town this summer looking at infrastructure upgrades. I can't help hoping it will happen. It would make such a huge difference..." Her voice trailed off then she shook her head and looked at Ainsley. "Meanwhile, though, we have to deal with what we have. Do you think you remember our systems? Because it would be a big help to have someone in the office who could hit the ground running."

Ainsley eyed the dark computer. "I think so? That type of memory seems to be intact, at least in other scenarios."

Priscilla nodded toward the desk. "Give it a try."

Here went nothing. Ainsley turned on the computer and watched it run through a familiar startup sequence. While the screen's wallpaper was new, the program names looked familiar. She glanced at Priscilla, who crossed her arms and nodded. Then she opened the two programs she'd used most often: one, a student database, and the other, a class schedule.

"Can you start Monday?"

Ainsley blinked and rotated the wheeled chair around. "Are you sure?"

"If you are. We can give it a trial run for a few weeks if you prefer, but I'd honestly rather not get someone else up to speed if I don't have to. Jenna will be out at least until Christmas — the twins are due around Thanksgiving — but she's not sure she wants to come back."

"I... thank you. My sister is with me until the new school year then she plans to return to Spokane, but I know she'll watch Bella for now. I do need a place to live, though. Right now, I'm with a friend in a one-bedroom apartment on the other side of Missoula, seriously cramping her style." And Ainsley's.

"If you can afford a damage deposit, there are some nice townhouses just a few blocks away. I happen to know one of my neighbors gave her notice on a three-bedroom yesterday. Her husband was transferred to Portland, and they're leaving before the end of June."

Two weeks. That wasn't bad. "My mother left me some

money when she passed, so if the rent isn't too high, I'm interested."

Priscilla glanced at the clock. "Let me give the property manager a call and see if they have a long waitlist or what the appropriate procedure is."

"Please." Ainsley held her breath. How were her prayers being answered one after another, just like that? She'd found Nathaniel before she'd even begun looking. Now she had her old job back, at least temporarily, and a lead on a place to live. *Thanks, God.*

Now all she needed was the rest of her memories.

NATHANIEL TAPPED AINSLEY'S NUMBER, and it went straight to voicemail. Again.

"When Dad gets a bee in his bonnet, he doesn't give much notice, does he?" Blake leaned on the corral beside Nathaniel. "I tried to call my girlfriend to let her know I have to cancel our plans for the weekend. Thanks, Dad. Right?"

"Yeah." Nathaniel stared at his phone. He had Carey's number, too, but he didn't really want to have this conversation with Blake listening in. Later. He shoved the cell in his pocket. "Cook's been busy with the prep and baking."

Blake grunted. "And we're stuck with the girls."

Maybe that would keep Nathaniel from spilling his guts to Blake. He definitely didn't need Alexia and Emma knowing his business. "Do they remember we don't have flush toilets in the highlands? This isn't going to go over well."

"Don't I know it. How did my father and your mother think this could possibly be a good idea? We're glorified babysitters with no amenities on top of eighteen-hour workdays."

"But we'll have tents." Nathaniel couldn't resist the dig.

"Hey, I tried. They're gonna hate it. They're gonna whine no end. One of us is going to end up escorting the princesses home early. Just watch."

"I don't know. They've been camping before. Noah takes them at least once a summer."

"It's one thing to sit by a lake with a fishing pole while you nap in the shade, and another thing entirely to be in the saddle every daylight minute for day after day."

"Don't I know it."

Blake eyed him. "You should talk to your mother and get her to rethink this. You know my dad will go by her decision."

"That'd be the day." Nathaniel scoffed.

"No, seriously."

"Yeah? I don't see how you figure my mother has any say in that marriage. They don't even share a bed. I don't know why she puts up with him at all."

"She's the one who moved out of the master suite, not him."

Was Blake seriously sticking up for Declan? Talk about a colt with blinders on.

Blake pulled out his phone and tapped, listened for a minute, and shook his head. "If Dad's looking for me, I'm off to town for a couple of hours. I can't catch Arlene on the phone, and I need to let her know I'm going AWOL. Promise I won't stay out late," he added with sarcasm.

"Four o'clock's gonna come mighty early."

"You think the princesses will be saddled and ready?"

"Yeah, I do. They're good kids, Blake. Remember what it was like being stuck up here before any of us had a driver's license and wheels? They're bored."

"Dad's idea of them learning to cook was a good one."

"You should learn, too."

Blake rolled his eyes. "Why? Cook's good at it. Someday I'll get married, and the little woman can keep the house."

Was that what had gone wrong in Mom's marriage to Declan? Nathaniel remembered life before cancer. His parents had been partners in the kitchen, with Dad busy on the ranch and Mom teaching school in town. Whoever could juggle the time cooked.

Mom hadn't taken over the meals at Rockstead. Cook had been ensconced in the kitchen for several years by then, since Declan's divorce from Travis, Blake, and Ryder's mother.

"Good luck with your little dream world." Nathaniel poked Blake's shoulder. "If you're headed to Jewel Lake, you better get rolling."

"Yeah. You need a girlfriend, bro. Didn't I hear Noah set you up with somebody?"

"He tried. Kyra's a total no-go." She had been even before Ainsley had walked through that door.

"Bummer. But there are other fish in the pond. Want me to keep an eye out?"

"No, thanks." He could just imagine the kind of woman Blake would consider suitable.

"Your loss." Blake sauntered off, jingling his keys.

After the truck rumbled down the drive, Nathaniel

pulled out his phone again. Another tap of Ainsley's number sent him straight to voicemail again. Then a message her mailbox was full.

Ainsley!

Had she run again, taking Bella with her? She'd promised not to, but if the person who threatened her resurfaced, Nathaniel couldn't count on her promise.

He also couldn't completely discount the wariness in her eyes. She didn't trust him, not completely.

He found Carey's number and tapped it. It also went to voicemail, like it was a conspiracy or something. Why hadn't he insisted on getting Carey's address? All he knew was that she likely lived near that park, and four apartment buildings towered over the small green space. All night wouldn't be long enough to buzz every unit.

Ainsley was going to freak out when she called, and he didn't answer. Just like he was freaking out now.

CHAPTER EIGHT

T his is pretty nice." Vivienne looked around the small but brightly lit space.

Ainsley set Bella on the floor, and the little one toddled off. Of course, they needed furniture, but she had some in storage from when she'd left town two years ago. It wasn't a lot, and it wasn't fancy, but it would help. Bella could sleep in the pack-and-play a while longer. Whatever Mom had left behind in Spokane probably belonged to Hector. Ainsley would rather hit a few thrift stores than ask him for anything.

Bella found the carpeted stairs and began clambering up.

A baby gate was going to be Ainsley's first purchase. For now, she followed the toddler up to find three small bedrooms and a bath.

"Dibs that one." Vivienne pointed at the one over-looking the street.

That was probably the master, but who cared? Viv

would only be here for a couple of months before returning to Spokane.

Ainsley nodded. "Sounds good. Bella gets the little one." She peered into a space not much larger than a walk-in closet. Still, it would be an improvement over the pack-and-play wedged against Ainsley's bed where the slightest twitch from one woke the other up.

That left her with the room whose window looked out into an enclosed green space the size of a postage stamp. She couldn't help smiling at the sight of their very own yard.

"You're going to take it, aren't you?" Vivienne asked.

"The rent seems reasonable, but it's a little bigger than Bella and I need."

"You can always make a home office after I leave." Vivienne looked out the window. "Besides, the yard."

"I know, right?" Already Ainsley envisioned Saturday morning coffee in a deck chair while Bella played nearby. "Yeah, I think I'll take it. The manager wants a six-month lease, and I have a job for that long, so… I'm in."

Vivienne grinned. "It's so cute, and so is the town."

"You could always stay, you know."

"Nah. All my friends are in Spokane."

They weren't the best influence in the world. Ainsley had to keep reminding herself she wasn't Vivienne's mother. Not that their own mother had kept that close an eye on either of them. "If you change your mind, just let me know."

"Deal." Vivienne hesitated. "Carey's nice and all, but her place is so small and not baby-proof at all."

"Trust me, I've noticed."

"So… can we move in today? I know it's early, but the people already left, and the cleaners have come. Why would the property manager mind?"

Ainsley studied her sister. This was the most interest Vivienne had shown in anything in quite a while. It would only take a phone call to the storage guys. Maybe they could deliver the pod today?

She cringed at the thought of all the money she was spending, but Mom had left enough to help with extra expenses like these, and she had a job starting Monday. Wouldn't it be easier — to say nothing of cheaper — to walk to work from here than commute from Missoula? And Vivienne would be so much happier out of Carey's apartment. "I'll see what I can do."

"Yay!" Vivienne picked Bella up and twirled her around the open space until the toddler giggled.

Ainsley's heart melted at the vision. What would she ever do without her kid sister? They'd never been close — twelve years age difference had seen to that — but in the past two years, they'd slowly been getting there. "I'm sure going to miss you," she blurted.

Vivienne settled Bella on one hip and raised her eyebrows at Ainsley. "You mean you'll miss having a babysitter."

"I'll miss you for much more than that. I'm so glad you're my sister. You're a great person."

"Aw, thanks." Vivienne turned and headed for the stairs. "I kind of like you, too."

That was a lot of bonding from Vivienne.

Now if only Nathaniel would call. It had been a few days since she'd heard from him. She hadn't expected this much silence, not after the intense way he looked at her and that random proposal. Maybe it hadn't seemed random to him — obviously, he had memories that she no longer shared — but he'd certainly shocked *her*.

Enough to make him rethink wanting to be involved with her and Bella? She couldn't line that up with his intensity. But with him or without him, Ainsley needed to step back into the world as a responsible adult with a child to care for. She was making the necessary steps now. A job. A home.

Lots of women raised kids by themselves. Mom had... but there wasn't much about her mother that Ainsley wanted to emulate, when it came right down to it.

"Ainsley? Your phone made a weird little sound," Vivienne called from the main floor.

Her phone? Ainsley scowled. It hadn't been working right for a while now. She jogged down the stairs, cringing as she remembered that wasn't the best thing for her head. She went to her purse where she'd set it by the front door as they came in, and dug her phone out. Nothing looked amiss. She jabbed a few buttons and discovered her voicemail.

Didn't that used to be on a more visible screen? There were unending messages from Hector covering the past week and a couple from Carey and Viv she'd completely missed. But her phone hadn't rung. Delete. Delete. Delete.

This was confusing. And all this frustration drew the darkness in again. No. She was *done* with the headaches. Except she wasn't.

"Viv?" She sat on the floor, drew up her knees, and held

out her phone. "Can you figure out why my phone hasn't been ringing?"

"You okay?" Vivienne crouched in front of her, concern on her face.

"Give me a minute." Ainsley cradled her head against her knees.

"Mama, mama." Bella patted Ainsley's shoulder and planted a wet smooch on her arm.

For Bella, Ainsley would do anything. She'd keep the panic away. *Lord, help me, in Jesus' name.*

"It was on silent mode." Vivienne sat beside her, shoulder to shoulder, thigh to thigh. "All notifications turned off. It should work now."

Had Ainsley set it to silent? She must have, but she couldn't remember doing so. Just one more missing memory drifting in the dark abyss where they all seemed to live. If only she could go fishing in there and find the ones that mattered most.

THE SIX HORSES, two of them loaded with camping gear, plodded along the trail in the high ranges. Nathaniel let the familiar movement lull him. Blake rode in the lead, with one of the packhorses trailing him. The twins came next then the second packhorse.

Nathaniel brought up the rear, counting on Kingpin's ears to alert him of any danger. Bears were common in the mountain meadows, but it was mostly a case of live and let live. A guy needed to be aware of their presence, though, especially if it was a sow and cubs. He mumbled again at the necessity of keeping Emma and Alexia safe.

Both girls rode well. Travis had put them in classes at the fairgrounds last summer. They'd learned some skills that might even be useful.

That didn't mean Nathaniel wanted to be responsible for them for the better part of a week. Who knew what went on in those conniving little heads of theirs?

Now that the trail had widened, Emma had drawn Desiree up beside Alexia's Domino. The two of them conferred. Alexia glanced back at Nathaniel.

He tipped his hat at them to remind them he was watching. Not that they were likely to seek an escape. This recon ride *was* their escape.

It occurred to him he'd never really sought to get to know his sisters. Not like Noah had done, and Ryder to some extent, as closest to them in age. Maybe that would change this week. Maybe they'd be a welcome distraction from Ainsley's silence, which sat like a niggling ulcer in his gut.

Hadn't they been down this road already? Smiles and sunshine one day and bleak silence the next? Even if she came back with, 'sorry, it was all a mistake,' he'd been well and truly reminded that he couldn't trust her. At least not until her memories had been restored and she recalled loving him.

What if that never happened? What if they were gone for good? He wasn't much for looking things up online, but he should make an exception for this. But exception was the keyword there. It didn't much matter if 99% of folks with TBI-induced amnesia had their memories restored; Ainsley could be that 1%. There was no way to know.

Did that mean he had to hold her at arms' length? That's where she wanted him right now. He'd been an idiot to take that ring along on Sunday, let alone flash it at her with the most unromantic proposal a guy could blurt out.

But… Bella. He had a daughter.

Alexia and Emma's laughter tumbled toward him on the breeze, and he couldn't help a little smile in return. They were so good with Travis's son, Toby. Emma, especially, loved to hang out with the five-year old. They'd take to Bella, too, wouldn't they?

He imagined bringing his daughter to the ranch. Imagined Mom making friends with her granddaughter, though she'd kept a bit of distance from Toby when Travis was so unfriendly. Things were better now.

Not necessarily better between Mom and Declan, but between everyone else since Travis and Dakota had mended fences and been married last fall. Travis had moved into Dakota's townhouse in Jewel Lake and drove up to Rockstead six days a week, sometimes bringing Toby with him.

Surely Travis wouldn't do that forever. It was a long drive, especially through the winter. Of all of them, Travis had ranching running most deeply in his veins. But… apparently Dakota made up for that.

Could Nathaniel do the same? Live in town and drive up every day? He could pool with Travis, probably. But what seemed like a distinct possibility a week ago now seemed vague. Why hadn't Ainsley picked up her phone in the day and a half he'd tried to let her know about this trip?

He blinked, realizing his sisters flanked him, and he hadn't even noticed. Great rearguard he was.

"We've been thinking about you," Emma began, glancing past him to her twin.

Uh oh. Nathaniel raised his eyebrows and looked between them.

"We think you need a girlfriend."

He shook his head, not that they cared.

"Our friend Beth has a big sister who works in an office downtown, but she likes to ride. We think you should meet her."

"Nope."

"But look how much nicer Adam and Travis are now that they're married. You could be nicer, too." Alexia waggled her eyebrows.

"If that's supposed to be the clincher, you need to learn some negotiation skills."

Emma twisted in her saddle to face him. "Deny they're nicer."

Impossible. "You're right. Travis, especially."

"See?"

Nathaniel grinned at her. "I didn't know I wasn't nice already."

Emma studied him. "You just poke along doing whatever. You hardly ever smile, and you're no fun at all."

"You used to be more entertaining," Alexia put in. "A couple of years ago. But that was sort of like one spot of sunshine in springtime. It only proved it was possible for you to smile at all."

The twins had noticed Ainsley had made him happy? That was information to tuck away and mull over later.

For now, though, he needed to nip their matchmaking ideas in the bud. And not give them any new ammo.

He grinned at one then the other. "See? I can smile."

They looked at each other and something passed between them. Twin-speak. He and Noah had once been good at that, as well, but they'd fallen out of practice as adults. Didn't help Noah was away from Rockstead so much with his itinerant blacksmithing business.

"You're faking," Alexia said. "We can tell when it's real and when it's not."

"We are experts on reading people," Emma added.

"Oh, yeah? Why don't you go read some Blake? He's only a year younger than me, plenty old enough to get married. And he's far more interested." Which was a bald-faced lie, but evidence did point that direction.

Emma wrinkled her nose. "He has a new girlfriend every week."

"I didn't even know there were that many women his age in Jewel Lake," Alexia added.

Nathaniel nodded. "Maybe he'll meet someone at the Pot of Gold Treasure Hunt this summer. He signed up, didn't he?" They'd know.

"Yep. I wish me'n Emma could, too."

"Emma and I," he corrected automatically.

Alexia's eyes danced. "We got Nat to admit he wants to do the geocaching hunt, Em."

"Nice try. I still think you should bug Blake. Just think of all the potential."

Alexia kneed Domino and trotted up beside Blake.

Nathaniel grinned as he watched them interact.

"We really do think you seem sad, Nathaniel," came

81

Emma's quiet voice from beside him. "Falling in love would cure that."

"Falling in love doesn't fix everything, little sis."

"You sure?"

"I wish I didn't know it so well."

She smirked at him.

Great. He'd given her the ammunition he'd promised himself not to.

CHAPTER NINE

Not bad." Carey set a box down on the floor beside the staircase. "You've got twice the space I do, and the rent is only fifty bucks a month more. I should be living in Jewel Lake and commuting into the city."

"I'd love to have you nearby. And I can't thank you enough for letting Vivienne, Bella, and me invade your space for two whole weeks." Ainsley offered her friend an impulsive hug.

Carey gave her a questioning smile. "That's what friends do. They're there for each other."

"Well, I appreciate it." Would Ainsley have done the same if the situation had been reversed? It was hard to be sure. Apparently, she hadn't even told Carey the name of the cowboy she'd been dating two years ago. Why had she been so secretive? The worry niggled.

"So, are you full-time then? How much work is there in a school office in the summer?"

"It'll be more like half to three-quarter time until the

first of August, then full-time." Too bad it wasn't the other way around, since she had a babysitter now. But this way she could spend more time with her sister before Vivienne returned to Spokane. It would work out. It had to.

Vivienne came down the stairs. "I just put a couple of towels over the curtain rail to darken Bella's room, and I think she's down for her nap. How can I help?"

"I don't know what I'm going to do without you," blurted Ainsley.

"You'll do fine. You're a good mom." Vivienne turned into the kitchen. "Anyone else hungry? I could fix sandwiches."

"Oh!" Carey whipped out her phone. "I haven't had takeout from the Golden Grill forever. Let me treat. Do you know if they do deliveries?"

"Reuben on rye." Ainsley's eyes widened. "I'm sure that's what I used to order there. Their food is so good! Right?"

"Reuben? I love those." Vivienne closed the fridge door.

Ainsley needed to get groceries. Her to-do list seemed a billion items long. Worry squeezed, and she tried to blink it away. She had enough money to tide them over for a bit. She could afford groceries.

But what if the voice belonged to someone from Super One? It didn't seem likely. But everywhere she went, she needed to be sure to see people before they noticed her in hopes of recognizing the man in time. She might only have seconds to react.

Maybe she should have stayed in Spokane.

Chicken.

At the same time, the threat seemed real, and she had Bella

to think about. But, no. She'd prayed. She'd made the decision. She was here. She'd already found Nathaniel… but why hadn't he called? Maybe he'd tried when her phone was on silent.

Maybe it was all her fault. Wasn't it usually?

"There." Carey flourished her phone in the air then stuck it in the back pocket of her shorts. "I'll go down and grab that in about thirty. And if it's half as good as I remember, I'll definitely look into moving back to Jewel Lake."

"There must be a physical therapy clinic here. Maybe you wouldn't even have to drive into the city for work."

"Worth a look. I do like my boss and my clients, though." Carey brushed her hands together. "I think we can get the rest of the pod emptied this afternoon if we stick to it."

Vivienne nodded. "Let's do it."

Ainsley blinked back tears. What had she done to deserve people like these two in her life? "Thanks."

Carey turned at the door. "You okay?"

"As okay as I get these days."

"You sure?"

"Yeah." Ainsley looked around at the few pieces of furniture and the stacks of boxes they'd pulled out of the pod. She had a bed and dresser left outside, but they wouldn't haul those up until Bella was awake.

"Look, why don't you start putting stuff away in the kitchen?" Carey studied her. "You know where you want it. We'll just bring the rest of it in."

Ainsley cut open a cardboard box and pulled out a silverware tray and other cooking utensils. Those were easy, since the small kitchen didn't have a ton of drawers. Look, one box down, eighty-nine thousand to go.

Twenty minutes later, Carey dropped the last box on the pile. "Viv and I are heading downtown to grab lunch. That okay?"

"Sure. Thanks." Ainsley opened another box. This one was full of paperbacks. Romance novels by some of her favorite authors. Multiple titles from Elizabeth Maddrey. A handful of titles from Melanie D Snitker and Valerie M Bodden.

She stroked the covers. *I remember these stories. I wonder if she ever finished writing the series?*

Where was a bookcase? Right, they'd put it in her bedroom. With Bella-the-busy on the loose, it seemed wiser. Quietly, Ainsley carried the box upstairs and set it in front of the small bookcase. Then, with great reverence, she carefully set each paperback in its place. But what was barely sticking out from the top edge of that book?

A photo she'd been using as a bookmark, which maybe meant she hadn't finished that one yet.

She'd taken this selfie. She remembered it clearly. She and Nathaniel had gone for a hike up Miner's Rock, and she'd wanted to capture the view behind them. She was smiling at the camera with the lake in the background, but Nathaniel… he was focused on her. The love shining in his eyes must be why she'd printed this one off her phone.

Ainsley's heart clenched as she stared at the precious image. This was what Nathaniel remembered. He remembered loving her in all the ways a man could love a woman.

Now she had some sort of real proof they'd been together, not just a general familiarity. Not just his say-so.

He'd loved her. She'd loved him back. But then she'd run away, not even taking this print with her. The digital file would have been lost when the taxi ran over her phone.

She flipped through the remaining paperbacks, but there were no more photos. No more images of Nathaniel to jog her memories. Maybe he had some on his own phone. She'd ask him when she next saw him.

Unless he was ghosting her like she'd done to him, just to show her what it felt like, but Nathaniel wouldn't do that.

Would he?

NATHANIEL SAT BESIDE THE CAMPFIRE. He should soon put it out and crawl into his bedroll, but instead, he tossed a few more small branches into it.

Mountains remained starkly silhouetted against the northwestern horizon, though the sun had set over an hour ago. Stars dotted the dark velvet above. A wolf howled in the distance, and the hair on the back of Nathaniel's neck prickled for a few seconds.

"Nat?" Emma whispered, creeping up beside him.

"Hey, can't sleep?"

The girls and Blake had rolled into their sleeping bags a while ago. Rumbling snores from over Blake's way proved he'd drifted off.

She sat close beside him. "Did you hear that wolf?"

Nathaniel draped his arm over his kid sister's shoulder. "I did. It's far away, Em. Nothing to worry about."

"I like hearing them from the ranch, when I'm safe in

my bedroom."

He grinned into the darkness. "Strong walls make a difference, don't they?"

"Yeah." Emma stared into the flames. "Fires are so mesmerizing."

"They are."

"Why are you still up? You have to get up as early as the rest of us."

He shrugged. "I need a bit of alone time here and there. Hard to come by when you're surrounded all day by other people."

Emma giggled quietly. "You make it sound like half the town's population is all around you. It's only half your family."

"I know." He picked up a thin branch and began breaking it into pieces which he tossed in the crackling flames. "I might be the most introverted person in that family, though."

"What's that?"

"Someone who needs silence and alone time to get up the energy to deal with people."

"Not me," Emma declared. "I get too much of that at Rockstead. I wish Mom and Dad would let Lex and me go to school in town."

"We were all homeschooled," he reminded her. "It's a long trip into town twice a day. Someone would have to drive you."

"Travis does it."

"The other direction, and only once a day, not twice."

"I still think—"

"Nothing I can do about it, sis. That's a parental decision, nothing to do with me."

Emma sighed heavily. "I know. But we're in high school, and we hardly have any friends except for at church. We almost never even get to go to youth group, even though Pastor Eli keeps asking us."

By the time Nathaniel had been fifteen, Adam and Travis had their licenses and drove the lot of them to youth group and gymkhanas and wherever else they wanted to go. Then the middle three — he, Noah, and Blake — had done the same for Ryder. He could almost spare some sympathy for the girls.

Almost. If he didn't hate being around people so much.

Not all people. Just multiples of them. Doubling from a family of three boys to six had been brutal on the heels of losing his dad. Declan had never seemed a father to him. To be fair, the man hadn't been much of a dad to his own sons, either, and he hadn't improved as the father of daughters. Surely girls needed a hands-on dad as much as boys did.

"You should ask Blake to take you in Friday nights. He's usually going anyway."

Emma leaned her head against Nathaniel's shoulder. "Lex asked Mom once, and she said he stays out too late for us."

"Probably true."

"I hate living at the ranch."

"But you like riding."

"Well, duh. But town kids can ride, too."

"Not any old time they feel like it. You and Alexia have a lot more freedom."

Emma sat up straight. "I bet we could ride into town."

Panic whirled in Nathaniel's brain. "Uh... that's probably a bad idea." The amount of trouble those two could get into unsupervised was pretty much unending.

"Yeah, I guess. A car would be much quicker. We could probably take the ATV down to the highway, and a friend could pick us up."

"Your dad would freak out if you left an ATV parked down there for hours." Nathaniel knew that for certain. Noah and Blake had once done it. They'd been grounded the rest of the summer.

"Duh. We'd hide it behind some bushes and take the key with us."

"We need the ATVs at the ranch ready to roll at any time."

"There's two of them."

"And seven guys. Get the idea out of your head."

Silence.

"If you don't believe me that it's a bad idea, ask Blake."

Emma sighed. "What will he say that's different? No one thinks about Lex and me. We're people, too, you know. And we're growing up."

That last sounded like a threat. Great. "Look, I promise I'll see what I can do about getting you to youth group sometimes. How's that?" Maybe if Ainsley wasn't finished with him for a second time because this time he'd ghosted her instead of the other way around, he could see her and Bella Friday evenings.

Having his twin sisters needing a ride back to Rockstead would help keep him on the straight-and-narrow. That wasn't all bad, considering their past.

On the other hand, it would be hard to keep knowledge

of Ainsley and Bella from the twins. What Alexia and Emma knew, everyone soon found out, and Nathaniel wasn't really ready to go there with the whole Cavanagh clan just yet.

"Youth group might be okay. I wouldn't even know."

"It used to be fun when we were teenagers."

"Did you have Pastor Eli, too?"

Nathaniel laughed. "No, of course not. He's about our age."

"Oh. He seems old."

Anyone out of high school seemed ancient when a kid was fifteen. Nathaniel remembered.

Emma nudged his arm. "Are you going to start dating so you have something to do when Lex and I are at youth group?"

"Sounds like a terrible reason to date, don't you think?"

"What are you so afraid of?"

He chuckled, keeping it quiet so as not to waken Alexia or Blake. "What makes you think it's fear talking?"

"When's the last time you went out? I can't even remember."

Nathaniel elbowed her back. "Why would I announce it to a pipsqueak like you?"

"Okay, then, how long?"

"A couple of years," he admitted.

"I don't know whether to be shocked you've ever invited a girl out, or shocked it's been that long. Are you figuring on being a monk or something?"

Ainsley's sweet smile came to mind, along with the blissful presence of his tiny daughter on his lap a week ago now. "Not a chance, Emma. Not a chance."

CHAPTER TEN

I t wasn't until late Monday evening that Ainsley's phone rang. Oh, she'd talked to Priscilla once over the weekend and exchanged a couple of conversations with Carey, but this — *this* was the call she'd been waiting for.

Nathaniel.

Unless he was calling to say haha, fooled you.

He wouldn't do that. She'd memorized that photo in the past few days. A man who looked at a girl like he'd gazed at her wouldn't be that mean. He wouldn't even know how.

Ainsley ducked up the stairs. "Hello?" she asked breathlessly.

"Ainsley? It's Nathaniel. I'm so sorry."

She let out the breath she'd been half-holding for days. "What happened?"

"Declan sent Blake and me into the high country for a recon trip, and I couldn't get a hold of you before I left."

See? She'd told herself over and over that it wasn't anything terrible, and she'd been right. "I had a setting wrong on my phone. Vivienne helped me figure out what was going on, but then I couldn't reach you." She still hadn't called Hector back, though. Whatever her mom's long-time partner wanted, she didn't care.

"I missed you so much."

Ainsley picked up the small photo. She'd tucked it into a frame yesterday so it could sit on her nightstand. Now she leaned back on her pillows and looked at it while talking to Nathaniel.

"I was afraid you'd thought better of me and gone back to Spokane."

"Not gonna happen," she said softly. "I got my job at the academy back and even found a townhouse for rent on Aquamarine Drive. We moved in Saturday."

"Wow. I'm sorry I missed everything."

"But you were working."

"I panicked for days because I couldn't reach you."

"I'm sorry. That was all my fault."

"I was worried I'd pushed you too hard by asking you to marry me."

Ainsley took a deep breath. "You caught me by surprise, is all."

"I'm sorr—"

"Nathaniel? It's okay." At least, she thought it was. "Remember that day in April we hiked Miner's Rock?"

"I remember like it was April this year instead of two years ago. Are you telling me you remember it, too?"

"I found a selfie I took of us. I'd printed it out and used it as a bookmark. I guess when I left, I just put all those things into storage."

"But you have a memory?"

"Yeah. There was a squirrel throwing pinecones at our heads. And then the wind came up before we got back to the car."

"You do remember."

She could hear the smile in his voice. "I do and, Nathaniel? Do you have some photos of us you could text me? Maybe that will jog more memories."

"I do. I'll send them tonight. I can't believe you're starting to remember!"

"It feels really good."

"Any more clues about the man who threatened you?"

The dark cloud pulsed a little. "None, but I've been trying not to focus on that. Because when I do, then I get really nervous. I'm trying to be watchful of people around me without letting the paranoia win."

"I find people hard all the time."

"I remember that about you."

"You do?" Wonder filled his voice.

"Is that why we didn't tell people about us?"

"Partly. I grew up with five brothers, one of them my twin. Frankly, I didn't have much that belonged to just me. Other than my horse."

Ainsley had to chuckle at that. "Why else did we keep us a secret?"

"I'm not sure." He paused. "It seemed important to you, too. Since I also wanted privacy, it was easy to agree. I guess I should have asked more questions. Probed a little more."

"You had no way to know you'd be the only one with memories."

"That's true."

She set the framed photo on her propped-up knees and gazed at the adoration on Nathaniel's face. "I've missed so much."

"We both have. Why don't you tell me about Bella? About your pregnancy — hey, were you ever in Saddle Springs that fall? Noah said he thought he saw you, but you didn't recognize him. Which, given the amnesia, would make sense."

"Saddle Springs?" Ainsley scowled, trying to remember. "I think I drove out once to take some files to a friend of my mom's."

"Most people would send them by email. Or Dropbox."

"My mom wasn't like most people." Wasn't that the truth?

"Was she a Luddite?"

"You mean someone who's against technology? No. She had a computer and used it." Ainsley's head hurt. "I don't know why."

"It's okay. Probably not important."

But what if it was? For right now, she had to stash that incomplete thought aside with all the other questions needing answers.

"Can I come see you and Bella tomorrow evening? I can bring takeout."

Her heart sped. He still wanted to see her. Still wanted to see his daughter. "I just went grocery shopping. Why don't you let me cook for you?"

"You're already working and taking care of a busy toddler. It's one way I can help."

"Well, if you put it *that* way…"

"Please let me, Ainsley. If I were better at it, I'd offer to cook at your house, but you probably don't want to be poisoned."

She giggled. "It couldn't possibly be that bad."

"You'd think."

"Okay. Vivienne probably wouldn't say no to a night off. I... I did tell you my sister is here with me until school goes back in, right?"

"Right. I'd forgotten. See, you're not the only one who can misplace a thought." Ainsley heard the smile in his voice. "Even someone without a bump on the head can manage to do that sometimes."

"Good to know."

"I'm happy to bring enough for her, as well. I'm so thankful you have someone there who can help you out. I'm sure you'll miss her a lot when she returns to Spokane."

"I really will." Ainsley glanced toward her bedroom door, but she'd shut it firmly. She lowered her voice, anyway. "I don't love all of her friends, so I wish she'd consider staying with me. On the other hand, I can't blame her for wanting to finish high school where she's been all her life."

"No, that seems reasonable. Will she live with her stepdad?"

"Hector?" A sense of foreboding about all those missed calls plowed into her. "It might be a possibility, but I doubt it. She was thinking more of her best friend."

And Ainsley needed to listen to Hector's messages and possibly call the man back, much as she didn't want to.

Nathaniel set the bag of fried chicken on the doorstep of the townhouse, shifted the vase of daisies to his other hand, and rang the doorbell.

It seemed a tidy, well-kept complex. That was a relief. He wouldn't be as worried about the neighbors as at her last place.

The door opened and there she stood. Ainsley Johnson, the most beautiful, most desirable woman he'd ever seen. She tucked a blond strand behind her ear and looked at him nervously. "Come in?"

All he wanted was to draw her into his arms and kiss her, but she wasn't there yet. He held out the clear glass vase. "These are for you, though they're not half as gorgeous as you are."

"Thank you." She took the vase from him and buried her nose in the petals. "They're beautiful."

Nathaniel picked up the food bag and followed her inside. The place was familiar and strange at the same time. He remembered the shabby sofa and the vintage coffee table. He'd sat on one of those chairs and eaten at that kitchen table. But it had been in a different apartment. A different life.

And then his daughter toddled into the room, and his heart nearly stopped. He set the food on the coffee table and crouched down. "Hi, Bella." Bella the beautiful.

He could hardly believe she was his and that he'd missed so much of her life. That ended here. He'd never be willingly parted from her again. Her and her precious mama.

The little girl stopped and stared at him, touching her

fingers to her mouth. And then she jabbered something he couldn't understand.

"What's that, Bella?"

Ainsley lowered herself to the floor nearby. "Use your words, Bella."

"Mama." Bella launched at Ainsley and fell into her lap.

"That was pretty clear." His arms itched to pull the pair of them close.

"She says half a dozen words. Mama and fifi are two of her best ones." Ainsley cuddled Bella for a minute before letting the little one go.

Once again, Bella stood staring at Nathaniel.

"Hi, little girl. I'm dada. Can you say that?"

Babble that may or may not have included *dada* tumbled out of Bella in a questioning tone.

He'd take it. "Good girl. I'm dada."

Then he realized they weren't alone. In the kitchen doorway stood a teenage girl with long hair a little lighter in color than that of his sisters. Did all teen girls look alike? He hadn't paid much attention to them since he'd been a teen himself.

He rose to his feet. "Hi. I'm Nathaniel. You must be Viv."

"Vivienne," she corrected, giving him a cool once-over.

Noted. "Nice to meet you. I'm so thankful you've been here for Ainsley and Bella. I really appreciate it."

Her eyebrows angled up, increasing the level of deja-vu. "I'm Ainsley's sister. Where else would I be?"

And, by implication, Nathaniel was the newcomer. Which, from the girl's point-of-view, was understandable. "That's great." He glanced around, his gaze landing on the bags of takeout. "Let's get started eating, shall we? Unless now doesn't fit Bella's schedule?"

The teen rolled her eyes. "She eats like eight times a day. It's never *not* mealtime in Bella's world."

"Sounds like an adolescent boy." He grinned at Vivienne. Maybe she had a boyfriend. Maybe she'd find that humorous.

Maybe not.

"C'mon, Bella." Vivienne scooped up her niece and buckled her into the highchair at the other end of the table. That had definitely not come over from Ainsley's previous apartment.

Nathaniel turned, but Ainsley had already picked up the takeout and was carrying it to the table. "Want to grab some plates from the kitchen?" she tossed over her shoulder to Nathaniel.

"Sure thing." He went past the table and into the small space beyond it. Where were the plates... hmm. Not that many options. He opened two cupboard doors before finding them then gathered up some silverware and went back out.

Ainsley edged past him in the doorway, so near he could feel the heat from her body and smell her green-apple shampoo. Snatching a kiss was a bad idea, but man, patience was getting harder and harder. "Just getting some glasses," she said hurriedly.

Vivienne gathered her hair together and tossed it over her shoulder then bent to pry the top off the bucket of chicken.

He chuckled.

She froze, angling slightly toward him with a glare in her eyes. "What's so funny?"

"Nothing." Nathaniel tried for a disarming smile, but it obviously wasn't working as intended. "You just remind me so much of my sisters. Mannerisms and all. I didn't realize teenage girls had so much in common."

Her eyebrows peaked then she gave her head just enough of a shake so her hair covered the side of her face as she finished the task. She pulled out a piece of chicken breast, picked up a knife from the pile he'd set on the table, and began carving it into tiny bits.

Of course. Bella couldn't eat a whole big piece of chicken. He should have thought about what she would like. How many teeth she had and all that sort of thing.

Ainsley set glasses on the table and then took a seat across from Vivienne, leaving the end for Nathaniel. He could sit and stare at his daughter the entire meal. It might be safest to do that, since Vivienne seemed prickly, and he wasn't sure where he stood with Ainsley.

Nathaniel cleared his throat. "May I ask the blessing?"

"Of course." Ainsley smiled at him and nodded to her sister. "Vivienne is nearly ready."

CHAPTER ELEVEN

All that animosity.

Ainsley could hardly stand Vivienne's antagonism toward Nathaniel. What had the cowboy ever done to deserve the teen's short answers and rolling eyes? Thankfully, Viv focused on Bella to the point where she met every one of the toddler's needs before Ainsley even noticed them. Like she was proving how indispensable she was.

Which was totally true. Every time Ainsley thought of managing without her sister after early August, she fought back waves of panic.

Nathaniel made small talk, but Bella couldn't answer and Vivienne refused to. That left Ainsley. Too bad she couldn't focus. She'd so wanted Vivienne to like Nathaniel. What did it mean that she didn't? Was there something negative about the cowboy that Viv saw but Ainsley couldn't?

Finally, Nathaniel lapsed into silence. Only Bella jabbered on between bites of French fries and little squares of chicken and the frozen green peas Vivienne had rolled onto her highchair tray.

When Viv finished eating, she pushed back her chair. "I'll give Bella a bath. Looks like she needs one." Then she scooped the toddler into her arms and headed upstairs.

Bella waved bye-bye over Vivienne's shoulder.

Now it was just Ainsley and Nathaniel. And, once again, discomfort bubbled like the foul contents of a witch's cauldron.

"I'll help you clean up." Nathaniel began stacking plates.

"You don't have to. It will only take a minute to do later."

"I don't mind." He carried the plates into the kitchen then called back. "Do you have a container for the rest of the chicken? It should make a good lunch for you tomorrow."

He was a good guy. Whatever Vivienne had against him, it couldn't be anything horrible. Ainsley's radar was on full alert, and she was picking up no negative signals.

Upstairs, she could hear bathwater running. She could trust Viv with Bella. For now, she could focus on the man who was her child's father. She carried glasses into the kitchen. "Thanks for texting me those photos last night."

Nathaniel turned to face her. "We had some really good times together."

"Seeing them helped me remember a little bit. Walking along the Clark Fork in Missoula. Weren't we buzzed by hummingbirds?"

His smile softened. "You remember! I picked a lily for your hair, but we had to throw it away when the hummers wouldn't leave you alone."

They'd stood in that flower garden and kissed. Had it been their first kiss? Either way, she remembered the warm sunlight and the pressure of his arms around her, holding her close, amid the fragrant lilies. She remembered the tenderness of his lips and the adoration in his gaze. But most of all, she remembered how he'd made her feel in the depths of her being.

She'd loved him.

She knew that now.

But was it wise to love him again? Maybe, in the depths of her being, she'd never stopped. The thick, black cloud of amnesia had hidden that knowledge from her, but it was dissipating, and the depth of her former feelings flourished in the newfound sunlight.

"Ainsley?"

She focused on his dear face, lined with concern and more than a little doubt, and set the glasses on the counter beside the sink. She was so close to him now she could feel the heat from his body. All she needed to do was turn, just a little.

"Nathaniel." Ainsley gripped his hands.

The worry lines smoothed away as he searched her eyes. "Are you okay?"

Define okay. She took a deep breath. "I remember that I loved you."

When his hands dropped hers then slid around her waist, she stepped closer and allowed him to gather her tight against him.

Ainsley nestled against his chest and closed her eyes. She smelled the faint fragrance of horse along with the aftershave he'd always worn, a combination that was all

Nathaniel and filtered deep into her awareness. She felt the softness of his worn denim shirt against her cheek and filled her fists with the same fabric around his back. She reveled in every point of contact between their bodies and the soothing sensation of his hands roaming her back. But not too soothing.

His cheek rested on the top of her head. She could feel his breath in her hair as surely as she could feel his heartbeat against her cheek.

She could have stood there forever, safe in the circle of his arms.

"I love you, Ainsley." His whispered words caught at the end. "I'll never stop loving you." Then his fingers tangled in her hair, tilting her head toward his.

She looked up at him. His face was so near. She slid her hands up his cheeks, and his eyes hooded over.

This man.

Ainsley stretched just a little and swept her lips across his.

"Are you sure?" His whisper sounded like a dying man uncertain if oxygen would be snatched away.

"Kiss me, Nathaniel," she whispered back.

His mouth covered hers, sweetly at first then more urgently.

The taste of him was flavored of home. She remembered — no, not all the details, but enough to recall the joy and light she'd always felt with him. He was *good*. There was no way at all that he was the person who'd sent her running.

The darkness pulsed around the edges, but she focused on Nathaniel. She'd worry about that again later. She could be certain of it — it would remind her over and over until the time came when she could banish it for good.

Nathaniel could help her. He was on her side. Hers and Bella's.

He threaded his fingers into her hair, his thumbs caressing her cheekbones. "I've missed you, sweetheart. Your heart is my home."

Heart and home. That sounded good. Perfect, even.

IT WASN'T the first time Nathaniel was thankful for the row of small log cabins along the creek on Rockstead. They were relics of a bygone era when Declan's grandfather had run the ranch, hiring a dozen ranch hands before ATVs and helicopters made the job so much easier.

He was also thankful that Declan had allowed his herd of sons and stepsons to move out of the ginormous mansion and populate these cabins, though Ryder had stayed in the main house much longer than the others, only moving into Travis's vacated cabin last summer.

Some days it was nice to come home and not risk seeing anyone. Nathaniel pulled the door to his cabin open, stepped inside, and panicked for a second before he recognized his twin. "What are you doing here?"

Noah looked up from his tablet over on the leather sofa. "I live here. Remember?"

"Well, yeah, but it's Tuesday. You're only here on weekends."

"Not this week." Noah stretched his long legs in front of him and set the tablet down. "Where've you been?"

Nathaniel hesitated. Did he have to talk? All he wanted was to cradle close the memories of kissing Ainsley. Of tucking his little daughter into bed. A pack-and-play, Vivienne had called it.

"Must have been a hot date," Noah drawled.

"She's remembering more and more stuff."

"That's good. Right?"

Nathaniel felt a sappy smile cross his face. "Yeah. We looked at some photos on my phone of things we did together a couple of years ago, and they jogged some memories. So, that's pretty amazing."

"Soon I'll have this cabin to myself, huh?"

Nathaniel laughed. "You know there's an empty one right down by Cook's. All you need to do is ask for it and move in."

"Do you want me to?"

"No." He took a deep breath. "Lack of accountability was how we got in trouble last time. Knowing you could be here any night of the week will help keep me in check."

"You didn't learn anything from conceiving a child?"

"Of course, I learned something, but it was something I already knew. The thing is, Ainsley and I had decided two years ago that we would save sex for marriage, but that decision didn't stop us. I guess... I'm concerned it could happen again. I don't want it to, but Noah? I don't want to wait any longer to marry her."

"Dude. She's been back in your life, what, two weeks? You don't think you might need just a little more time to get to know each other again? She had a big knock on the head. Maybe some personality changes and all that."

"Doesn't matter. She's Ainsley. She's the mother of my

child. There's nothing she could say or do to make me change my mind about her."

"Dangerous words, bro. You do remember someone was threatening her, right?"

"Yeah. But I can protect her from whoever that was."

"So, you're packing heat and will pull it on the guy?"

Nathaniel skewered his twin with a glare. "If I need to. You don't get it, but she means *everything* to me. And I do mean everything."

"That's a dangerous place to be." Noah held up both hands. "Because the only one who should mean everything to you is Jesus. I'm glad she's back. Don't get me wrong. I'm glad you two have a chance to talk things out and see where you can go from here. I'm glad you have the chance to know your daughter — hey, I'm an uncle!"

If that was supposed to divert Nathaniel, it wasn't working. He crossed his arms and stared at his brother. "I didn't mean she was more important to me than God."

"But hear your words, Nat. They came from your heart."

"So what if they did? Do you think God put testosterone in guys' veins so we'd sit back and let others push our girls around? Nuh uh. Not on my watch."

"Nat, all I'm saying is to make sure you're spending time in the word. Make sure you're praying about every step you take with Ainsley."

"I am." But was he, really? Or was he going mostly by a strange combo of emotion and logic? Because logic certainly dictated that he take care of his family, and wasn't that by marrying his child's mother? Especially since they were in love.

Even Ainsley was remembering that. Soon she'd love him again in the present, not just remember loving him in the past. And then he'd pull out the diamond ring again and do a better job of asking her to marry him. He'd set up something a little more elaborate like he'd begun to plan two years ago, but still befitting two people who liked their privacy.

Whether or not he'd propose to Ainsley wasn't the question. The question was only when and how. How could God's will be otherwise? It couldn't, plain and simple.

It would be best if she'd remember the strange man's threat first. Nathaniel would like to wipe the worry from her sweet face so she wouldn't need to carry that burden ever again. But if a few more weeks went by and she didn't remember, that wasn't going to keep him from stepping into the future. The two facets belonged to different timelines.

"If you're serious about Ainsley, you should bring her to meet Mom."

"I'd rather take Mom to town."

Noah laughed. "Do you know when Mom last went to Jewel Lake that wasn't a Sunday morning? Or have you even noticed she hardly ever goes to church anymore?"

He'd noticed. Nathaniel eyed his twin. "Do you know why?"

"No idea. I hate to interfere, but I'm really worried about her. I think she'd like to meet Ainsley and Bella, though."

"I did tell her about Ainsley, but I didn't know about my

daughter then." The words still tasted strangely on his tongue.

"She's Mom's granddaughter," Noah said quietly. "I think it will be a big deal to her."

"I'm not sure… it's just that the last time I saw Ainsley back then was up here. When she drove off the ranch that morning, that was it for two very long years."

"You afraid you'll lose her again? You're some kind of crazy, Nat. If you're that worried about her, then you definitely shouldn't propose."

"No, it's not that." Nathaniel frowned and stared down the hallway unseeingly. "It's… what if the man who threatened her was from the ranch? What if it was Travis or Adam or…?"

"Declan," they said in unison. They shared a look.

"It's a possibility, I guess," Noah said at last. "It had to be someone, and he's the kind who'd get in someone's face and push buttons. Remember how he and Monica got into that shouting match last summer?"

"No one who was within five miles of the corrals that day could forget." Nathaniel shuddered. "That cursing had a lot of volume."

"What did Ainsley say the guy said?"

He scrunched his face, trying to recall. "'I know who you are, Ainsley… Go. Don't come back.' And other things she can't remember."

"What could he possibly have meant?"

"I wish I knew, Noah. I wish I knew."

CHAPTER TWELVE

I t's not fair," blurted Vivienne. "How come Bella gets to have a dad, and I don't?"

Ainsley crossed the space and sat beside her sister on the mattress on the floor. "I get it, but we have to start somewhere."

"But Bella doesn't even know what she's missing yet. When I see how Nathaniel looks at her, I wonder if my own father even knows I exist. Why doesn't he love me?"

"Mine, too."

"I hate Mom." Vivienne clutched her pillow to her chest. "Why did she have to sleep around like that? Why did she refuse to tell us who our fathers are? Didn't she *know* how much it hurt? Didn't she care?"

Ainsley slid her arm around her sister's shoulders. "I can't answer that. I've always wondered, too."

"It's not fair." Tears streaked down Vivienne's face.

"I don't know what I would have done without God as my Father."

"It's not the same thing. Didn't you see Nathaniel tonight? He couldn't take his eyes off Bella."

"I noticed, all right." Ainsley's heart felt raw at her sister's grief. "But I imagine God looks at us like that, too. There's a verse in First John — here, let me read it to you." She thumbed on her phone and found the reference. "Chapter three, verse one. 'See what great love the Father has lavished on us, that we should be called children of God! And that is what we are!'"

Vivienne plucked the phone from her hand and read it through a few more times.

"I know how hard it is to not have a dad, Viv. You know I do. But if I had to choose between an earthly father and a heavenly one, I'd take God every time. He will never let us down."

"Is it wrong to want both?" Vivienne leaned against the wall and closed her eyes.

"No, it's not wrong."

"You were eleven when I was born, right?"

Where was this going? A niggle of something twitched in Ainsley's gut. "Yes."

"And you didn't know whom Mom was spending time with?"

Ainsley racked her brain. That era was much clearer than the past couple of years, but she'd only been a child herself. "Mom worked for Carey's dad here in Jewel Lake. He sold insurance. Life insurance and other types, I think."

"Could he be my dad?"

"Maybe? I don't think so, though. You and Carey aren't anything alike. But the Andersons did get a divorce around that time." Could she just flat-out ask Carey if her father had ever had an affair with his secretary? Would Carey even know?

Vivienne eyed her. "You and I aren't much alike, either. You're blond, and my hair is darker. You're thin like a wisp, and I haven't been since I was ten."

"That's not conclusive."

"Then it isn't conclusive that Carey's not my sister, either. At least we know our mom and her dad knew each other."

"Also true."

"Why did Mom move to Spokane before I was born? Maybe my father wasn't from Jewel Lake at all."

A headache began pulsing around the edges of Ainsley's brain. "I was so young. I don't remember knowing Mom was expecting until you were born." She squeezed Vivienne's shoulders. "But I did know she wasn't the average nourishing mommy. When I held you for the first time, I vowed you'd always feel loved."

"Thanks." Vivienne leaned against Ainsley. "You've always been there except for those months when you moved away. Mom was so angry with you, but she wouldn't talk about it. That meant I couldn't talk about you. Then you came home, and you were so upset, and then I kept walking in on you and Mom fighting, and then you'd both zip up silent but keep glaring at each other..."

"Oh, Vivi. I'm so sorry."

"What was she so mad about, anyway?"

"I wish I knew. A few weeks ago I thought it was because I'd come home pregnant, and she wished I hadn't taken after her like that."

Vivienne angled to look at Ainsley. "But that wasn't it, was it?"

"No, because when I do the math, I didn't even know I was expecting when I went back to Spokane. There was some other reason…"

"Maybe you'd found out who my dad was?" Vivienne's face brightened with hope.

I know who you are, Ainsley… Go. Don't come back.

"I hate to burst your bubble, but I'm pretty sure it wasn't about you. It was about who *I* was."

"But you don't know." Vivienne shrugged away.

"I don't. I've asked God so many times to restore the rest of that memory, but so far, there's only one tiny flicker. It's just not enough to go on."

They sat in silence for a few minutes. Ainsley looked around the makeshift bedroom. "I'll buy you a real bed with my first paycheck, and let's look for a dresser we can paint or restore, too."

"Doesn't matter. I'm not staying."

"I'd like it if you did."

"Just because you want a free babysitter."

"Oh, sweetie, is that what you think? Yes, Bella will miss you, but it's way, *way* more than that. You're my sister. We've only got each other."

"Until you marry Nathaniel. Then what will become of me?"

Ainsley twisted on the mattress to face her sister fully. "Is that what's worrying you? That choosing Nathaniel means rejecting you?"

Vivienne rolled her eyes at the same time as she sniffled.

"Sweetie, it's not true. If I marry Nathaniel, you'd be more than welcome to live with us. I'm never turning any sister of mine away. I want us to be close forever."

"Did he say to bring your kid sister along? I doubt it. Besides, who'd want to live with newlyweds? Not me. Not even for Bella's sake."

"Ouch." Ainsley added a dramatic hand on her chest to demonstrate the pain, but it was real nonetheless. "I mean it, Viv."

"Yeah, well, whatever. I'm going to live with Stacy until I graduate. And then I guess I'm on my own."

"When you change your mind, I'll still want you, whether it's next week or next year."

Vivienne pushed out a huge yawn. "Oh, wow, it's my bedtime. Nice chatting, sis."

Ainsley squished the teen to her side. "Love you, kid. See you in the morning."

"Yeah."

She peeked in at her sleeping toddler on the way past. Bella lay on her tummy, her diapered bum upthrust. Ainsley smiled as she tucked the blanket around the little one. "Sleep tight, Bella Babe. I'm glad you know your daddy."

"THIS IS A BAD IDEA." Ainsley backed away from Nathaniel, both palms extended.

He kept his smile in place. He'd worked with skittish fillies before. All it took was consistency and a calm demeanor. "Bella is my mom's only grandchild. She wants to meet her."

The panic hadn't left Ainsley's face. "She can come here."

"She... has some issues and rarely comes to town. Meeting her at Rockstead is best."

"I-I can't."

"That's why I'll drive. We'll stay an hour, max, and then I'll bring you right back to Jewel Lake. I promise."

She shook her head.

"We won't go anywhere near my cabin." Was that what was bothering her? "We'll park by my mom's garden and visit there for one hour. Then we'll get in the truck and come back."

"Nathaniel..."

"Trust me." Which maybe was a laugh, because he hadn't proved trustworthy with her two years ago. Things were different now, in so many ways, but her fear was palpable.

It just didn't make sense that the threat had happened at the ranch. Nathaniel's brothers wouldn't ever say something like that, which only left Declan. And that didn't make any sense, either. Yeah, the man was full of himself, but a personal threat to his stepson's girlfriend? That was above and beyond.

No, the threat had to have come from someone else in town later that day. No matter how many times Nathaniel tried to reconcile what had happened, it was the only thing that made sense.

"I bought a car seat for Bella, same brand as the one in your car. See?" He stepped aside, gesturing into the truck.

She shook her head, the only movement she seemed capable of at the moment.

"Travis always had a seat for Toby in his truck long before he and Dakota were married. It seemed such a good idea that I copied him." Which meant that his days of keeping Ainsley and Bella to himself had just been numbered, since eyebrows would rise at the sight of a baby seat in his vehicle. Whatever. The time for transparency had come… and introducing them to his mother was the first, most vital step to that transition.

Nathaniel tucked Bella into the seat. It took him a few minutes to figure out all those straps and buckles. When he was pretty sure he'd nailed it, he looked over at Ainsley again. "Did I do this right?"

"Nathaniel, I'm scared."

Right there on the driveway in front of her townhouse, he wrapped his arms around her stiff body and held her until she finally leaned against him. "I won't leave your side, not even for a second. I promise it will be okay. My mother's going to love you. She can hardly wait to meet you both."

"What if…?"

"What if what, love?"

She shuddered against him. "What if I remember something I don't want to?"

Wasn't restoring her memories exactly what she needed? Wanted? Her question didn't even make sense, but he bit back the words that told her so. Probably wouldn't go over well.

"I'll be watching out for you, love. I promise." He opened the truck door and helped her up.

Bella babbled from the backseat. "Mama!"

"Hey, Bella Babe."

Nathaniel let out a slight breath himself at Ainsley's response, though he could still hear tension vibrating in her voice.

They drove up to Rockstead in near silence, though he pointed out the road that led to Running Creek along with a couple of other highlights. He heard Ainsley's sharp intake of air as they rounded the last curve, and the large ranch house came into view. He turned aside before they reached it and angled down the grassy lane to the back entrance to his mother's garden.

He glanced over at Ainsley. "Ready?" She wasn't. He knew she wasn't, but he needed to push her, just a little, regardless. Didn't he? Or had he made a terrible mistake?

Too late. He could see the top of Mom's straw hat coming this way amidst the shrubbery. Nathaniel unbuckled Bella and swung her to one hip then held the truck door for Ainsley.

"I love you," he whispered.

She offered a tremulous smile and wiped her hands down her capris. "No matter what?"

"No matter what."

"Nathaniel?" His mom's voice came from the garden.

He turned the three of them around to face her. "Hi, Mom. I'd like you to meet Ainsley and our daughter, Bella. Ainsley, this is Kathryn. My mother."

"Oh, you sweet girls. Come in." Mom's eyes seemed suspiciously damp as she filled her gaze with the wispy-haired toddler.

Ainsley clutched his hand as they entered the enclosed

space. His mother led them into the heart of the garden where Noah had built a wrought-iron gazebo beside a little raised pond.

Nathaniel eyed the water. It wasn't very deep, but he'd need to keep a close watch on Bella. He set her down on the paving stones, and Mom sat on the pond's edge.

"I can't tell you what this means to me." Mom dabbed a tissue at her eyes. "Please, sweet Ainsley, tell me all about yourself. I feel like I've missed so much."

So had he, but the question had been directed at Ainsley.

Bella reached for a tall plant, and Ainsley lunged to stop her.

"Maybe we should go inside?" Nathaniel suggested. His mother's living space was austere — her preference — and there was much less trouble for a toddler.

Mom eyed Bella. "Probably a good idea." She led the way to the French doors to the basement level. "Please, come in. I dug through storage for a few toys leftover from when the twins were young. I hope Bella will like them."

"I'm sure she will." Ainsley picked the little one up and cast a wide-eyed question at Nathaniel.

He focused on radiating peace and confidence as he touched the small of Ainsley's back and escorted her in.

She perched on the edge of the gray sofa and, after a quick glance around for Bella-sized trouble, Nathaniel sat beside her, gripping her hand.

"Nathaniel says you work at Creekside Academy?"

"Yes." Ainsley glanced at Nathaniel. "In the office. I'm surprised how much there is to do when school won't be back in session until mid-August."

"I used to teach there when the boys were young."

"Oh, I'm not a teacher. Just an office worker."

"The heart of the school, where everything gets done to keep things running smoothly."

Ainsley relaxed a little. "That's true."

"I taught middle-school history and geography back then. Getting six horse-crazy boys through homeschool graduation was quite a challenge after that. Now the girls have three years left. I'm sure Nathaniel told you about his sisters."

She nodded. "Another set of twins."

"Yes. Fraternal twins seem to run in my family."

A sharp tap sounded on the door that led to the main part of the house.

Ainsley tensed. So did Nathaniel.

Mom rose and walked over, though. "That will be Declan. I thought it would only be right for him to meet you both, too."

The grip on Nathaniel's hand was enough to render his fingers paralyzed. This was definitely not okay with Ainsley. It wasn't okay with Nathaniel, either. Hadn't he told Mom how skittish Ainsley was? He knew he had.

The door opened, and Declan stepped in. His gaze swept the room, not even pausing on the toddler before bouncing off Nathaniel and laser-focusing all its force on Ainsley.

Declan's eyes narrowed.

And Ainsley crumpled to the sofa, only held up at all by Nathaniel's grip.

CHAPTER THIRTEEN

Ainsley fought for consciousness. This was her worst nightmare come true, the darkness taking over just when everything became clear. But she couldn't move. Couldn't *anything* but listen.

The man spoke, and it was definitely the voice she remembered. "What's wrong with her?"

Nathaniel's hand held hers firmly, grounding her. "She had a traumatic brain injury a couple of years ago, and there's a lot she can't remember. Sometimes the input is so overwhelming that a headache blindsides her, and she passes out. I'm not sure what caused it, but she'll be okay in a few minutes."

She'd never be okay again. The memories tumbled over her like snowmelt over a waterfall. There had been more, much more to that encounter beside the corral at dawn two years ago. Oh, it had only been words. The man — Declan Cavanagh — hadn't touched her. He hadn't needed to.

It was like she was right there, all over again...

"Who'd have guessed Saint Nathaniel would have a woman sleep over?" The man's voice had been derisive.

She knew who he was by reputation. Declan Cavanagh, Nathaniel's stepfather. She raised her chin but didn't answer him.

He blocked the driver's door of her car as he stood there, boots planted in the dirt beside the corral, sinewed arms crossed over his broad chest. A stare pierced right through her. "Who are you?"

"Ainsley." She cleared her throat. "Ainsley Johnson."

Something hardened in his gaze. She wouldn't have thought it possible. "Brenda's daughter?"

How did this man know her mother? She nodded.

"Your mother worked for Jason. What does she want now?"

What on earth? Now her gaze riveted on his. "What does she…?"

Declan's laugh was low and harsh. "Let's put it this way. What she and Jason were doing wasn't exactly ethical, no matter what she told you, but I took care of things. If you know what's good for you, you'll leave Jewel Lake and forget this ever happened. You and my stepson have no future together. The knowledge would crush him."

She glanced back at the bend in the lane. Trees hid the row of little log cabins where Nathaniel and some of his brothers lived. She'd kissed him goodbye, long and lingering. He wouldn't know he needed to come to her rescue.

Ainsley straightened her shoulders. "I love Nathaniel, and he loves me."

The man rolled a muscled shoulder. "That's just hormones talking. You'll get it out of your system. I know who you are, Ainsley. Just as importantly, I know who your mother is. Not only a tramp, but covering up Jason's tracks. Don't think I'm going to let your presence slide. Go. Don't come back."

Declan kept his gaze fixed on Ainsley's face as he opened the car door for her.

Relief warred with fear. She had to edge far too near the man to get into her car, but he didn't touch her. He shut the door firmly behind her and tipped his cowboy hat at her over his piercing eyes.

He stood in the same spot, still as a statue, staring after her until the bend in the driveway shielded her from his penetrating gaze.

And now, two years later, he was in the same room as her. She'd returned, right to his very own turf, just as he'd expressly forbidden.

Ainsley didn't even want to open her eyes, sit up, and deal with the situation. Could she stay still long enough for Nathaniel to call an ambulance?

But meanwhile, his stepfather would be feeding him misinformation about her. About Mom.

That's why she'd gone back to Spokane! To confront Mom regarding Declan's veiled accusations. Mom had hedged. Ainsley had probed. She hadn't been completely convinced her mother wasn't lying, but Declan had told Ainsley too little. Or too much, depending on which way she looked at it.

But Mom had convinced her to take a brief break from Jewel Lake and Nathaniel. Ainsley had quit at the academy and paid for her things to be put in storage, fully intending to get to the bottom of the vague and conflicting information, clear things up, and return to Nathaniel.

She'd missed her period. Bought a home pregnancy test. Positive. She'd been so distraught and distracted she'd stepped out in front of that taxi.

Crash.

The truth was supposed to set her free, but it didn't appear to be working. The bands around her head, around her chest, and around her knees seemed to constrict, cutting off all air and all hope of mobility.

She now remembered, but at what cost? Even Nathaniel couldn't save her from Declan.

But what, exactly, was so terrible she and Nathaniel and Bella couldn't escape together? Yet, Nathaniel loved ranching. She couldn't imagine him cooped up in an office or working in a shop. He needed to be free to ride the ranges with a horse between his knees and the wind on his face.

If he were free, she couldn't be. If she were free, he'd be tied.

She couldn't ask that of him.

The truth had definitely not set her free. It had only made the invisible bonds visible.

Ainsley should never have returned to Jewel Lake to find the missing years.

NATHANIEL NEARLY WEPT with relief when Ainsley's eyelashes flickered. He ran his hand up and down her arm. "Hey, my love. I'm here. It's okay."

She seemed to shudder beneath his touch. Maybe that was a normal response to awakening from a faint. He hadn't passed out once in his life, so he wouldn't know. "Ainsley."

He glanced over at Bella, who sat on the floor playing with an old telephone toy that had been Alexia's favorite years ago. The toddler seemed oblivious to her mama's condition. Probably just as well.

Mom and Declan had been whispering furiously at each other over by the door, but Declan's voice began to rise. "You don't understand."

"Because you've been keeping things from me."

"You didn't need to know. You were grieving."

"And that made it all right?"

"Jason—"

"He only wanted me for Joe's insurance, Declan. I saw right through him."

"There was more."

Nathaniel lurched around at those three words. He shouldn't have, because now his stepfather seemed to realize they had an audience. The man's face shuttered.

"What kind of more are we talking about, Declan?"

Nathaniel couldn't remember when his mother had sounded more clear. More deadly. He hadn't heard that tone since the time he and Noah had shot their BB guns at the goats. Mom had not been amused at their efforts at target practice, though the goats hadn't been harmed.

"Nothing. I didn't mean anything by that."

"I'm sure you did."

Declan glanced at his wife, then scanned over Nathaniel, Ainsley, and Bella before looking back at her.

"Nothing that matters anymore, Kathryn. It's all water long beneath the bridge."

"Maybe I'd like to be the judge of that."

This was what Nathaniel had been waiting to see for years: his mother standing up to Declan. But now that it was actually happening, he had a sick feeling in his gut, because it was related to Ainsley.

The truth punched him in the solar plexus, and he nearly doubled over. Declan had to be the person who'd threatened Ainsley. Something about knowing who she was.

Declan had tried to split up Nathaniel and Ainsley because of... whatever this was he refused to talk about. Something about Dad's insurance. And more.

Nathaniel surged to his feet, managing to lay Ainsley on the sofa rather than dumping her on the floor.

The startled toddler wailed.

He scooped her up, but she screamed louder, kicking and flailing at him. Great.

Nathaniel advanced on Declan. He could probably take the guy, but not with a bucking baby in his arms. And maybe he couldn't. Declan might be thirty years older, but he was extremely fit. "What are you talking about? How does this relate to Ainsley?"

Mom pivoted. "To Ainsley?" She looked past him to the woman struggling to sit up on the sofa.

It was like Mom had just realized Ainsley held a key, that this conversation would never have happened if there wasn't a history between Declan and Ainsley.

"Bella Babe?" gasped Ainsley.

Nathaniel set the kicking tot on the floor, and she

scrambled to her mama. Ainsley gathered her close, and the screaming ceased instantly. The silence was nearly as deafening as the noise had been.

"Declan, I think you've got some explaining to do." Mom's harsh voice grated like an ice saw.

"Kathryn—"

"Now, if you please."

The man swallowed. Once again, his gaze made its circuit before he focused back on Mom. "Maybe we should speak in private."

She shook her head. "Nathaniel's right. Somehow this has to do with Ainsley. I want to know how, and I suspect Nathaniel does, too."

Declan drove a hand through his hair, closing his eyes for a brief second.

Nathaniel had never seen his stepfather so far from large and in charge. Pity tried to well in him, but no. He needed answers before he could determine which emotion to allow rein. "Let me start. Two years ago, you threatened Ainsley, didn't you? Why?"

"You don't want to know. Trust me. You don't."

"Trust you?" Again, Mom stepped up before Nathaniel could. She might be six inches shorter than Declan and sixty pounds lighter, but she looked a force to be reckoned with. "I think that ship has sailed, and you weren't aboard."

"Some things are best left in the past." The man didn't sound nearly as sure of himself as even five minutes ago.

Nathaniel stepped up beside his mother. "Blackmail? Criminal charges? What are we talking here?"

"Kathryn, please. I was only trying to protect you from Jason. Joe trusted him far too much, even in hospice. Jason tried to get Joe to sign new insurance forms where he was the beneficiary instead of you. Joe even signed one of the pages before he took a closer look and realized what his brother was doing to him."

Mom's eyes flashed fire. "That weasel. But where do you come into this?"

Good question. And one Nathaniel wanted the answer to, as well.

"I confronted him. He laughed at me and said he'd win, anyway. He'd marry you and get Running Creek."

"Like I would have let him." But Mom's voice trembled.

"He wasn't going to make it optional."

Nathaniel tucked his hand around Mom's elbow in solidarity. "How did *you* find out?"

"I had ways." Declan looked just past Nathaniel's head, not quite making eye contact.

Clickety-click. Pieces fell into place. Ainsley's mother had worked for Uncle Jason. But before Nathaniel could voice his thoughts, Ainsley came up beside him, jiggling Bella. "You told me you'd taken care of things," she accused. "What did you mean?"

This was a new detail. Had Ainsley remembered more? Or had she been withholding information all along? Had she only befriended Nathaniel in the first place to get information from Declan?

"Look, Jason wanted the ranch. His business was doing poorly because he was a lazy fool who took the easy way out. He'd started looking for widows to fleece and thought his sister-in-law was fair game. He'd get Running Creek, find some way to get Kathryn's name off the deed, and sit on Easy Street for a while."

"You… you… I can't…" Mom's voice broke.

Nathaniel could fill in the gaps. "You weren't any better. You married Mom to get your hands on Running Creek yourself. How's that any better than my uncle Jason?"

"I… loved her?"

"You lied to me." Mom was in his face now. "I thought we'd agreed to be business partners, but you withheld that information from me? I didn't have everything I needed to make a good decision."

"Jason was going to take the ranch from you, Kathryn. You and I have shared everything."

Things were moving too quickly. Nathaniel's blind-sided brain scrambled to catch up. There only seemed to be one thing to latch onto in all that. "You thought my mother was stupid enough to marry Dad's brother? Is that really how little you think of her?"

Fire flared in Declan's eyes again. "He wasn't going to take no for an answer."

"Why did no one think a woman could run a ranch by herself?" Mom demanded.

"Kathryn, this is ancient history. Seventeen years. At the time, you agreed."

"I thought you loved me! Now I find out it was to keep Jason's mitts off Joe's and my ranch because you didn't think I could handle him. But that doesn't even make sense. You just wanted the land yourself."

"I think it's high time you let Adam and Riley move onto Running Creek," Nathaniel heard himself say. "Or Ainsley and me. My brothers and I want our dad's ranch back."

"It was *my* ranch," Mom said fiercely. "Not yours."

Declan sucked in a breath. "There were big liens against it. I paid those. Kathryn, I did this for you. I've given you everything."

Everything, my foot. "She's been a hostage here for years."

"Would you mind your own business?" Declan's fierce gaze turned on Nathaniel. "Your mother is not a prisoner. She goes to town whenever she wants. You think it's my fault that's once a month instead of once a day?"

Nathaniel stared hard into his stepfather's eyes, holding his breath, waiting for his mother to clarify.

But when she spoke, it was not on that subject. "How did you find out Jason's plans? From Brenda Johnson?"

Ainsley's mom.

And in that instant, two things happened. Nathaniel heard his truck engine rev at the same time as he realized Ainsley was no longer by his side. The French doors were wide open.

Ainsley and Bella were gone.

CHAPTER FOURTEEN

Let's add Grand Theft Auto to my list of sins.

Ainsley jounced down the long driveway. She hadn't meant to steal Nathaniel's truck, but it was right there with the keys in the ignition, and she'd needed to get away from Declan's lies and forbidding presence.

Probably Declan would come roaring down the lane and force her off the gravel. He knew this road far better than she did.

She glanced in the rearview mirror and pressed harder on the accelerator. But when the pickup skidded around a sharp curve, barely holding against the sheer drop-off, she knew she had to slow down and risk being caught. She couldn't jeopardize her daughter's life.

Oh, Mom! How could you!

Because it seemed apparent that her mother had been part of Jason's scheme. Didn't that increase the odds that Vivienne was Jason's child? The thought curdled Ainsley's stomach. Was Jason planning to marry Kathryn and then divorce her and marry Mom, who carried his love child?

But that sounded convoluted for someone as lazy as Declan suggested.

How could Mom love a crook like Jason? Not that her taste in men appeared to be impeccable. Maybe it was just as well Ainsley didn't know who her own father was. Maybe she didn't really *want* to know, after all. Not if he was a creep like Carey and Vivienne's dad.

Ainsley had been back in Spokane for two months before the accident. She'd tried that entire time to break her mother's secrets open, but to no avail. Finally Hector had pulled her aside and told her to leave it be, that she was distressing her mother, who'd done nothing wrong and didn't deserve a combative daughter.

Hector.

What did he know?

Ainsley had deleted her entire voicemail box without listening, but he'd called a few times since then, too. She'd ignored those.

Why was he so insistent on talking to her? She hadn't ever been close to him. He'd been peripheral to her life, even though they'd lived in the same house most of Ainsley's high school years. He rarely spoke. Rarely even interacted with Mom in front of Ainsley or Vivienne, let alone with the girls directly.

Now, suddenly, he wanted to talk?

Huh. He might even have something important to tell her. Maybe she should pick up Vivienne and head straight for Spokane. Uh… she should take her own car, though. Not Nathaniel's truck. No need to add more sin to her account.

Nathaniel was never going to forgive her, anyway.

A sob broke out of her as she neared the highway. How could she bear to leave him behind again? She'd had such high hopes the past couple of weeks. He seemed to adore Bella.

She couldn't rip the man's child away from him. It might even be illegal. Not that stealing his truck wasn't. Not that what her mother and Jason had done had been right.

The web was tangled, and Mom had died before the threads began to unravel. If only Ainsley hadn't been struck by that taxi and forgotten what she needed to know from her mother, but maybe Hector held some of the puzzle pieces.

The road forked, the one side angling back toward Running Creek Ranch, while the main road led to Jewel Lake. Ainsley had never seen Running Creek — and today wasn't the day — but had her mother really been part of trying to wrest it from the hands of a grieving widow with three young boys? What had been in it for Mom?

She turned toward town, but a rumble from behind her caused her to look back to the Rockstead lane, where a cloud of dust tried to outrun the black pickup rapidly gaining on her.

Declan? Or Nathaniel? She couldn't face either.

Ainsley couldn't outrun them, either. She pulled to the side of the road, pressed her face into her hands, and braced her feet on the floorboards. What had she done? She'd acted without thinking.

She'd done that two years ago, as well. Just run in response to Declan's harsh ultimatum. There were so many things she hadn't known. Still didn't know. For everything that had become clear in the past hour, more hidden pieces now lurked in the shadows.

The black pickup veered in front of her, cutting off the road to Jewel Lake. Dust enveloped the cab where Ainsley sat.

Lord, I've made a mess. Over and over and over again. Can I blame the fact that I don't have all the information? I'm reacting, rather than acting.

Yeah... no. No one had forced her to steal Nathaniel's truck. That had been an action. She couldn't blame anyone else.

The cab door wrenched open. "Ainsley?"

It was Nathaniel, his harsh voice lacking the warmth and tenderness she loved so much.

She swallowed hard and glanced over, taking in his firm stance and piercing gaze.

"Dada! Dada!" Bella babbled from the backseat.

He opened the rear door, unclipped Bella, and lifted her into his arms. "Hey, baby girl."

There was the sweet tenderness, directed at their daughter, not at Ainsley. But the toddler had done nothing wrong. She hadn't withheld information, hadn't run away, hadn't pushed Nathaniel's love aside. Her mama had done all that.

"Talk to me, Ainsley. What was going on back there?"

"I... remembered some stuff."

His eyebrows peaked. "Like?"

"It was Declan all along. He threatened me that morning, but he was vague, and I needed more information. That's why I went to Spokane. To talk to my mother and find out what was true."

"You quit your job, emptied your apartment, and closed your social media accounts. That's not what people do when they want a bit of info from their mother."

Tears pulsed down Ainsley's cheeks. "If they feel threatened, they might. I did."

"Seriously? What did he tell you?"

"He… he said…" Ainsley tried to recall the exact words. "He said what my mom and Jason did was wrong, but he took care of it. He told me to get out of your life, that… that the knowledge would crush you."

"The knowledge would crush *me*? Since when does Declan care about my feelings?"

"I can't answer that."

"Ainsley, you don't know Declan. Not like I do. There's never been a tender little father-son bonding moment between us. He doesn't care what crushes me or lifts me up. I'm ranch labor to him. That's it."

Her chin came up. "Then why do you stay? Come with me. Let's go far away from whatever his secret is, his and Jason's."

Nathaniel shook his head. "I can't leave my mother in his clutches. And besides, that revelation *was* his big secret. That he married my mother to protect her from Jason, as though she needed his interference."

"There's more."

His eyes bored into hers. "Oh? Like what?"

Ainsley reached for her daughter. "Come to Mama, Bella."

The toddler giggled and burrowed her face into Nathaniel's shoulder. He'd only known his little girl for a couple of weeks, but she'd won his heart in the first five minutes. At least holding their daughter would keep Ainsley from running for now. "I've got her."

Ainsley's eyes flashed. "She doesn't even know you."

"Like I don't know *you*? Ainsley, talk to me." He was trying to be patient here. "What makes you think there's more to the story?"

Her gaze skittered from his before returning.

She was lying about something. *That* was the knowledge that crushed him. But he couldn't get all soft and mushy as though it didn't matter. It did matter, and she needed to know it.

"He called my mom a whore."

Nathaniel closed his eyes for a second, jiggling his daughter, who giggled.

"You've basically said the same thing to me," he said at last. "That you and Vivienne have different and unknown fathers. That your mother was living with some other guy when she died."

Ainsley cringed.

But seriously, she was protecting her mother's reputation? The woman had made her own decisions, and the evidence was all right there. It didn't mean Ainsley was like her mother, any more than Nathaniel was like Declan.

"He said you'd hate me because of my mother." Ainsley clenched the steering wheel, making Nathaniel glad he was blocking her getaway with Adam's truck.

Nathaniel had spent most of his life resenting his stepfather. Not hating him as Adam had done, but neither had there been lost love. He'd taken his cue from his mother's withdrawal, unable to help her, but equally unable to abandon her. A helpless boy who'd grown into a defensive, watchful, silent man. "I don't think your mother has that much power over me," he said at last.

"He said she covered up Jason's tracks."

"My uncle was a sleazy opportunist. He's nothing but scum."

"He's my best friend's father."

"If Carey thinks her father is a great guy, then it's just as well my family has little to do with hers since my dad passed."

"Don't you get it? Blood is a strong tie, at least for those of you who know the relationship. Carey and Laurel went with their mom after the divorce, but that doesn't mean she hates her father. You can love someone you're related to even when you don't really like much about them."

"Like you and your mother."

A tremulous smile appeared. "Exactly. She wasn't an easy woman, but she was my mom."

Nathaniel shifted Bella to his other arm.

The toddler squeezed his cheeks and giggled. "Dada."

His heart all but melted. It would turn him into mush if he didn't need to stay strong to get to the bottom of this thing with Ainsley.

"So, she worked for Jason and was in league with him. Did she think she was going to raise you on Running Creek after she helped Jason get rid of my family?"

Ainsley's eyes grew wide. "I have no idea what she was thinking, but it wasn't that!"

"Are you sure?"

"Hector... I have to talk to him. He's been trying to get in touch with me, and I've been ignoring him. I wonder if he holds the answers to any of my questions."

"You're good at avoiding people you don't want to talk to."

"Hey! I had a TBI."

Nathaniel watched her squirm. "I think we've confirmed that your accident wasn't for two months after you left Jewel Lake. For two months, you could have phoned, texted, or emailed me at any time. You didn't. I understand the injury and the brain damage, but what about the time in between?"

Her mouth opened and closed a couple of times as she stared back, looking for all the world like a deer caught in the headlights.

His heart sank. "You didn't love me enough to talk to me. I was planning a bright future with you, but you walked away without a second glance."

"No, that's not it. I loved you. I did."

"Right now, you're thinking about running back to Spokane to talk to Hector, just like two years ago you returned to get answers from your mother."

That was guilt on her face, wasn't it? He pressed on. "I'll tell you what, though. I can't stop you. If you don't love me enough to stay"— he swallowed a hard lump — "I can't make you. I never want someone to stay with me out of obligation, like my mother has with Declan. But here's the thing."

Ainsley bit her lip as she dashed tears from her face.

He hardened his heart. There was only so much abandonment a guy could take, after all. "You're not taking Bella from me. She's mine, Ainsley, and if you run, you'd better leave her right here with me. I'm not even kidding you. Cowboys have figured out how to do their job with a baby on their backs before. You want to stick around? That's great. We're fifty-fifty on this parenting thing. But you don't get to take her from me."

"I can't even believe you'd threaten me like that. Like Declan did."

"It's not remotely like what my stepfather said to you. He didn't have a relationship with you. He was trying to protect his own butt from my mom finding out what he'd known before their marriage. Things *your* mother was trying to do to my family."

"It wasn't my mom! It was your uncle."

"Sounds like they worked together. I'll be talking to my brothers and my mom and see if we can lay charges against Jason even though it's seventeen years later. Too bad your mother isn't here to be charged along with Jason."

Her hands fisted and her face darkened, probably with the effort of not lashing back.

Nathaniel wanted to hurt her. Not physically, but emotionally. Because of her mother's relationship with his uncle, he'd lost the opportunity to grow up on his parents' ranch. He'd become a Cavanagh, without a choice to say no and remain an Anderson. Though with Jason's legacy, he wasn't sure the Anderson name was much better.

The point was, the option had been ripped from him right after a huge loss, and he hadn't even known.

What was Mom going to do now? He'd left her in heated argument with Declan. Knowing the man's fierce anger, Nathaniel feared for her safety, but he'd had no choice but to track down the woman he loved and the child they shared.

But as much as he loved Ainsley — and he did, didn't he? — could the reverse be said? Because how could a woman who loved him back keep running away from him?

CHAPTER FIFTEEN

Y ou can't cut calves for branding with a baby on your back." Holding Diesel's reins, Declan stared hard at Nathaniel.

"The girls can watch Bella on days she wouldn't be safe with me."

"They don't exist to be your babysitters."

"You've never objected to them watching Toby."

"Travis had enough sense to leave his child with Dakota during the workweek."

Nathaniel shifted Bella to his other arm. It was definitely true that Rockstead wasn't a safe place to turn a toddler loose. But what was his stepfather's problem about the twins? Alexia and Emma were bored out of their skulls now on their summer break. Much as they complained about being homeschooled, at least they were busy then. One of these days they were going to figure out they could, in fact, ride horseback all the way to town, and then there'd be no containing them. Heaven help them all when the twins were old enough for their driver's licenses.

"Don't shirk your work." Declan's gelding snorted and backed up.

Nathaniel shook his head. "When have I ever? I'm not about to start, just because I have a child."

"Ainsley—"

That did it. "I've had enough of you interfering in my relationship with my daughter's mother. You think you're God, but you're not."

"I can fire you."

"Go for it." *I dare you.* Nathaniel stared straight into Declan's eyes.

Bella grabbed both Nathaniel's cheeks and pulled. "Dada!"

Maybe Ainsley had the right idea. The three of them could leave Jewel Lake and go elsewhere. Nathaniel could get a job on some other spread. His twin knew a lot of ranchers in the region. Or maybe he should go to college and... do what? He'd been crazy about horses since he was Bella's age. He'd never wanted anything other than the great outdoors. Maybe he should have thought ahead a little more.

"Don't tempt me." Declan mounted Diesel and pivoted away.

Huh. Nathaniel had called his stepfather's bluff and won. Interesting that he didn't feel the elated satisfaction he would've expected.

"What was all that about?"

Nathaniel turned to see his brother Adam nearby, staring after Declan on Diesel as they pounded out of the yard. "We need to talk."

Adam eyed him. "The we that is you and me?"

"Don't sound so surprised."

"You keep to yourself a lot."

"This might be bigger than the two of us. Might take all six."

Adam looked from Nathaniel to Bella and back to Nathaniel. "Where's Ainsley?"

"Long story that's somewhat related."

"Okay. Then, yeah, we need to hear it. But all six? You know Declan's sons will stick up for him."

"I'm not so sure about that."

"Man of mystery." Adam jabbed Nathaniel's shoulder, which made Bella giggle. "She's sure a pretty little thing."

"She is." Nathaniel swallowed hard against the welling emotion as he patted his baby's ruffled backside with his work-worn hand.

"One of these days, Riley and I want to start a family." Adam sounded wistful. "Maybe we should rent a place in town like Travis and Dakota, but it hardly makes sense when we both work here at the ranch."

"I told Declan it was time to let you guys move onto Running Creek."

Adam blinked as he reared back. "You what? And what did he say?"

"That's part of the long, convoluted story."

"Okay, okay. Quit dropping hints. I'll drag the brothers together as soon as I can, then you spill everything. No holding back, you hear me?"

"I'm done with secrets."

"That'll be the day, Mr. Secrets."

"I'm serious." If only Ainsley had talked to him two years ago. If only she were talking to him now, but things had been pretty stiff between them the last couple of days since the confrontation. Only Bella kept him going back for more of Ainsley's snubbing.

No. Secrets weren't a good thing. His brothers needed to know what Nathaniel knew, even if his knowledge was incomplete. The situation between Mom and Declan affected all six sons. No one seemed to have guessed that the parental relationship had recently fractured even more deeply. After all, Cook often took a tray downstairs to Mom's rooms rather than setting a place for her at the family table. This had been going on for several years now, so the added rift wasn't particularly noticeable.

Even if Ainsley seemed incapable of being completely truthful, Nathaniel wasn't going to fall into that trap. Didn't the Bible speak of the truth setting people free?

Yep. That's how he was going to live. Starting now.

AINSLEY PACED THE TOWNHOUSE, aware of Vivienne tracking her movements more than the pages of the paperback in her hands. Ainsley's arms felt empty. How could she have acquiesced to Nathaniel's demand for more time with Bella?

Yeah, it was his right. She got that. But did he understand how trapped she felt? She couldn't go to Spokane without Bella... but why? Wouldn't it be easier? Hector had little use for the toddler. If he'd ever smiled in Bella's direction, Ainsley had missed it.

Nathaniel didn't trust her. That was the bottom line. And she couldn't completely blame him. She'd made one little comment about Hector's phone calls and Nathaniel had jumped to the conclusion she would run away again.

She wouldn't.

Would she?

Well, not without Bella, so Nathaniel was more right than she'd like to admit.

"You need to talk to Hector."

Ainsley had already nearly forgotten Vivienne was in the room.

"You're not going to have any peace until you figure everything out."

And, by extension, Vivienne wouldn't have peace, either. Fair assessment. "I can't just call him. He's the master of the monotone. I couldn't hope to read his voice on the phone."

"It's two days until the weekend. Go then."

Ainsley stopped and stared at her sister. Why had she been assuming all or nothing? It was less than a four-hour drive, a comfortable and easy weekend trip. She didn't have to abandon her job to get answers.

"But... Bella."

Vivienne sighed. "He wants to play daddy? Maybe he'll change his mind if he has her for the whole weekend and can't just drop her back to you when she gets cranky."

"I don't want him to change his mind." Not about being in Bella's life. It would be nice if he changed his mind about assuming the worst of Ainsley, though.

She deserved it. She deserved every bit of caution he was sheltering himself with. He said he loved her, but what was love without trust?

Nothing. She could see that now.

If only she hadn't taken the easy way out by taking his truck while Declan was rampaging. She'd felt like she was the only one who understood what that man was capable of. She'd had to protect Bella.

Hadn't she?

She looked at her sister. "You'll come with me, right? There and back?"

Vivienne rolled her eyes. "Of course, both directions. School doesn't start for another six weeks."

"I wish you'd stay. I could talk to Priscilla. The kids of staff members enroll at the academy for free. Maybe she'd let my sister, too."

"You just want a built-in babysitter." But the accusation didn't sound as vehement as the last time she'd said it.

"For my active social life? Not hardly." But Ainsley did need to start looking for a daycare spot for Bella once Vivienne was in school. "Think about it. Maybe check out the youth group at Creekside Fellowship on Friday night."

"Not if we're going to Spokane."

"You know? We could leave Saturday morning and still have plenty of time. I don't envision spending hours and hours having a heart-to-heart with Hector."

"You'd put off leaving for me?"

"Sure. Why not?"

Vivienne closed the paperback and set it aside. "I don't know. What if the kids here don't like me?"

"What's not to like?" Ainsley's heart skipped a beat. Was Viv really considering staying? "I know I'm biased, but I think you're the greatest teenager on the planet."

"Yeah... I don't know. Meeting a bunch of strangers

doesn't sound that fun. They all have their BFFs already and don't need another one."

"Maybe. Maybe not. Give it a try?"

"I'll think about it." Vivienne surged to her feet and strode into the kitchen. "Want some popcorn?"

"Sure. Sounds good." Ainsley stared out the window. The TBI-induced amnesia had been horrible. The headaches had hung over her for two years, especially problematic whenever she'd pushed hard to remember anything.

Now, she almost wished for them back. Ignorance had been bliss... except that it hadn't. What had been true paradise had been the past few weeks, falling in love with Nathaniel all over again. Until the final pieces fell back into place.

The truth hadn't set her free. Instead of settling her unanswered questions, it had opened Pandora's box and let loose a tumult of issues she hadn't even suspected.

Could she ask Nathaniel to keep Bella for an entire two days plus the night in between? He wanted to be a daddy, but Bella wasn't going to be easy at bedtime without her mama. Still, if Ainsley couldn't win Nathaniel back and he kept to his determination to halve Bella's care, he'd find out soon enough. Maybe sooner was better than later.

At least, with Vivienne's suggestion, Ainsley didn't need to worry about her job. She'd promised Priscilla the school year, no matter what. If she bailed on that agreement, she'd never get a good reference.

The microwave hummed in the kitchen, and the popping of kernels began.

Like it or not, Ainsley needed to be a responsible adult.

Bella counted on her mama. Vivienne counted on her sister. Priscilla counted on her office secretary.

And what about God? What about the verse she'd quoted to Vivienne the other day? She might not know her earthy father, but God was enough. She'd clung to so many scriptures over the years. Now Psalm 68 came to mind.

Sing to God, sing in praise of his name, extol him who rides on the clouds; rejoice before him — his name is the Lord. A father to the fatherless, a defender of widows, is God in his holy dwelling.

Ainsley wasn't a widow, but she might as well be if the rift remained between her and Nathaniel. But had God defended Kathryn, or let her be duped by a man like Declan Cavanagh? How had Kathryn thought he loved her?

Obviously, things had seemed different seventeen years ago, because Ainsley couldn't imagine how Kathryn could believe the man for two minutes.

What part had her mother really played in that foiled insurance scam? Mom hadn't actually done anything illegal, had she?

Hector. Maybe he had answers. At least some of them. Should she call ahead and give him time to evade her questions, or should she take a chance on surprising him?

Maybe the first step was actually listening to some of the voicemails he'd left.

"Ainsley? Here's the popcorn. We could maybe watch a movie?"

She blinked the condo back into focus. A movie sounded so normal in the midst of this entire mess.

"Sure. You pick."

For a little while, she could avoid the fact that Vivienne

would soon be moving away, that there were so many unknowns on the heels of the revelations she'd thought she wanted.

All she wanted was a daddy to offer advice and unconditional love. The only one who could do that was God, and she'd been struggling to keep up her end of the relationship. Didn't it go both ways?

But God had gone all the way for her. Sent His Son to die for her so she could have an unhindered relationship and life eternal with the Creator of the universe. Anything she could do in return seemed so... small.

He hadn't asked for big things, though. Just time together. Just her love and delight.

Thank You.

CHAPTER SIXTEEN

Ainsley waited outside Creekside Fellowship at ten Friday evening, tapping her fingers on the car's steering wheel. Transferring Bella to her crib later would be a small price to pay for encouraging Vivienne to get out and meet some local Christian teens.

Sue her if she wanted her sister to stay in Jewel Lake. Friends were going to be vital to that, and all Ainsley's current hopes lay in the church's youth group. Surely there'd be a girl or two willing to add a friend. Or a cute guy who might catch Vivienne's eye. Someone. Anyone. Well, nearly anyone.

A black pickup pulled in beside her car. She caught her breath, but instead of Nathaniel, the driver was his twin.

Ainsley frowned. She'd only met Noah once back then. She and Nathaniel had kept their relationship a secret from nearly everyone, avoiding Jewel Lake on their dates. They were both very private people, but they had nothing on Ainsley's mom.

A tap sounded on her window. Startled, she glanced in

the backseat, but Bella slept. She pressed the button to slide the window down a little.

"Hey. I'm Noah."

The cowboy looked a lot like Nathaniel, but they definitely weren't identical. His eyes, though... they pierced like his twin's.

"I remember."

"I hear things are rough right now, but I want you to know that having you back in his life means all the world to my brother."

Rough? Now that was an understatement. Ainsley forced a smile. How much did Noah know?

The guy leaned down a little and peered in the back window. "Is that my niece? She's sure a cutie."

"Yes, that's Bella."

"I won't ask you to wake her up for me."

"Good. Because I wouldn't."

He grinned, meeting her gaze. "I can't wait to get to know her. Nathaniel says she's coming for the weekend. You, too?"

"I..." What did Noah think? That she and his brother were sleeping together again? "No. I have to make a quick trip back to Spokane to get some information from my stepfather." And Nathaniel refused to let her take Bella with her, like he was holding their toddler hostage. No, she wasn't thinking like that. He had a right to time with his daughter, and he'd protect her. Ainsley believed him on that.

Hector hadn't revealed a whole lot on the phone, just as Ainsley had suspected of the stoic man. But there was a small box for her when she was ready.

Ainsley was more than ready.

Noah's gaze switched back and forth between Ainsley and her daughter, like he didn't know what else to say but didn't want to simply walk away.

"What brings you here tonight?" she asked.

He glanced toward the church doors. "I'm picking up my sisters. Between us guys, we try to make sure they have a ride to and from youth most weeks. Living so far out of town is a bit rough on such social butterflies."

"I can see that." Nathaniel had said he was the most introverted of all the Cavanagh cowboys, but Noah didn't look a lot more outgoing as he shifted from one foot to the other.

The doors opened and a flood of teens poured out, maybe thirty or forty in total. Ainsley held her breath. Of all those kids, surely one or two had extended a friendly smile to Vivienne.

Finally she picked her sister out of the crowd flanked by two girls. That was a good sign. Relief slid through Ainsley.

"Hey, there they are now. It was nice meeting you again, Ainsley." Noah straightened and walked toward the trio.

She frowned. The girls with Vivienne were the Cavanagh sisters? Did they know who Viv was? The relief turned to unease. After another peek at Bella, Ainsley opened the car door and moved to where Noah stood with the three girls.

"Hey, Viv. Ready to go?"

Vivienne turned and smiled at her. "Hey, sis. I'd like you to meet my new friends, Emma and Alexia. They're twins!"

"Hi. I'm Vivienne's sister, Ainsley." She smiled at the girls. Did she have to explain who else she was?

"And Nathaniel's girlfriend," put in Noah. "Peek in the back window at their little girl, Bella."

"Ooh!" exclaimed the shorter of the two girls as she followed orders. "Look, Lex! She's adorbs."

The other teen studied Ainsley for a minute before following her sister's lead. In seconds, both girls were peering into the car gushing with baby-talk.

But that wasn't what caught Ainsley's attention most. Looking at the twins' profiles niggled her with a sense of deja vu. On the other side of her, Vivienne turned to reply to something Noah had said.

Ainsley heard nothing. All her senses tingled with a new revelation. Vivienne looked as much like Emma and Alexia as they looked like each other.

But surely that was a coincidence. All three teens wore their hair long and parted slightly on the side. The Cavanagh girls' hair was brown, while Viv's was lighter, though not quite blond.

Any additional similarity was chance. That was all. Because there was no way that Mom had slept with Declan Cavanagh. Hadn't there been evidence she'd been involved with Jason Anderson? It was more palatable that Vivienne was Carey's half-sister than Alexia and Emma's. Would that make Vivienne Nathaniel's half-sister? No. He wasn't actually related to Declan. Thank the good Lord for that.

Ainsley forced her voice to remain level. "Ready to go, Viv? I need to get Bella in bed."

"Sure." Vivienne rounded the car. "It was great meeting you two."

"Same!" exclaimed Emma. "You'll have to come out to the ranch and go riding with us sometime soon. How about tomorrow?"

Ainsley's blood chilled. If her inklings were correct, she needed to keep her sister away from Declan.

"Can't this weekend. Ainsley and I are going to Spokane to see our stepdad. But we'll be back Sunday night. Maybe next weekend?"

"That'd be great," put in the other twin. "Have you ridden much?"

Vivienne shook her head. "Just a couple of times at camp, but I liked it."

The twins exchanged a look. "We'll find a good horse for you. Don't worry."

"I look forward to it!" Vivienne slid into the passenger seat.

The twins clambered into Noah's truck beside them with a wave as Ainsley backed out of her parking spot. "You had fun, then?"

"Yeah. It was pretty good. Pastor Eli seems like a decent guy."

"Excellent." Should she say something to her sister about the weird thoughts that had run through her head? No. Not until she had more evidence than a bit of similarity in their looks.

"Ains?" Vivienne spoke as they pulled into the driveway.

"Hmm?"

"Is it weird I feel like I've known Alexia and Emma forever?"

"Uh… a bit? Because that would put them on par with Stacy, who has been your best friend since kindergarten."

Just a couple of hours ago, Ainsley had been trying to think up any excuse for her sister to stay in Montana. Now, she couldn't wait to push Vivienne back to Spokane. Because the thought of Declan was just… no.

"I know." Vivienne laughed. "It does seem strange. And, of course, we've only known each other a few hours, so there's a lot we haven't talked about. I just know that I feel like I could tell them anything. Anything at all, and they'd understand and wouldn't make fun of me."

Ainsley reached into the backseat and began unbuckling Bella, holding her breath lest the toddler awaken. "Maybe don't start with your deepest, darkest secrets right off the bat, though."

Her sister chuckled. "And here you're always after me to make friends."

Friends, yes. With Declan's daughters? Not so much.

IT HAD BEEN A VERY long day.

Nathaniel had envisioned a happy child toddling around his cabin calling him *dada* and offering winsome snuggles. He'd gotten the opposite: a sobbing, soggy mess who spent hours crying for her mama. At nap time, he'd tucked Bella in the portable crib Ainsley had sent along, but the wailing hadn't ceased. Finally he'd taken her out to see the horses again, the only time all day she hadn't arched her back and screamed at him.

She was already horse-crazy at her tender age. His daughter, for sure, not that he'd doubted her lineage for a minute.

Served him right, probably. He'd insisted Ainsley leave their toddler with him, like he'd been afraid he'd never see either of them again if she didn't. Truth… but he still hadn't been prepared.

His five brothers filled the tiny living room in the cabin Nathaniel shared with Noah. This weekend his twin was bunking with Blake, since Bella had his room.

"Let me have her," Travis spoke into a brief lull.

"You've got a way with babies?" Ryder asked, jabbing his older brother with an elbow.

"More practice than you, twerp." He looked at Nathaniel. "Seriously. Give me a shot at settling her down, or we won't even be able to hear each other talk. And I, for one, want to hear your story."

Nathaniel held up both hands. "You're welcome to her. I changed her. Gave her a bottle and some of the food Ainsley left her. Jiggled her. All she does is yell."

Travis shook his head and marched down the short hallway. Bella's screams loudened when he opened the door then cut off abruptly a few seconds later. He came out a minute later carrying the toddler, who rested her tousled head against his shoulder, hiccupping around the thumb stuck in her mouth. Tears streaked her cheek.

Nathaniel felt nearly as miserable. He was such a failure. He'd like to be blazing jealous at his stepbrother, but at the moment, he'd rather kiss the surly cowboy who'd managed the miracle of blessed, merciful silence.

Travis stood at the end of the hallway, swaying and patting Bella's back. He poked his chin toward Nathaniel. "Start talking. I don't know how long this will work."

Five sets of eyes focused on Nathaniel.

Argh, he hated the limelight. "So, this is about our parents."

None of the brothers blinked.

Forward, then. "We all know theirs isn't a marriage any of us want to mimic. I've never understood why my mother married Declan to start with, let alone stuck with him."

Blake's eyebrows flickered. Maybe Declan's sons had a different view on the marriage than Kathryn's sons did.

"Anyway, our uncle Jason was a life insurance salesman. It turns out Ainsley's mom was Jason's secretary at the time our dad died. It came to light a few days ago that Jason had rewritten the terms of Dad's insurance and tried to get Dad to sign it. It would have named him as Dad's beneficiary and cut Mom and us boys right out."

Adam narrowed his gaze. "There's proof of this?"

"Verbal only. I heard Declan say it himself."

"Declan? What did he have to do with that?"

"My dad wouldn't—" interrupted Blake.

Nathaniel held his hands up. "Dad wasn't as far gone as Jason hoped, and he didn't sign the papers. But Declan... pointed out to Jason the error of his ways. He found out that Jason intended to get his hands on Running Creek one way or the other. If not through the insurance or the will, then through marrying Mom and *then* cutting her out."

"Mom's not stupid enough to fall for slime like Uncle Jason," Noah asserted.

But she'd been stupid enough to fall for Declan. Nathaniel didn't dare say that out loud, not in the presence of Declan's sons. He needed the six of them on one side, not divided by ancient history.

Bella sagged against Travis's chest, her thumb drooping from her mouth as she slept. Nathaniel was going to have to learn the ways of baby whispering from Travis.

Nathaniel turned back to the other brothers. "No. I'm sure she would have held her own just fine, but Declan made her an offer she couldn't refuse. I'm not sure what all was in that offer, but they agreed on a business partnership. One thing, it effectively cut Jason right out of the picture. That was success, I guess."

"So, she married Declan for protection from Jason?" Adam frowned. "That doesn't even make sense."

"They must have loved each other once," Blake added. "Our sisters had to come from somewhere."

Adam shrugged. "Sex doesn't require love."

"Well, no. I get that. I just thought… I remember better times. Don't you all?"

"Sort of," Nathaniel conceded. "But that was a long time ago. I'm honestly not sure their marriage can withstand this revelation. I've never seen Mom stand up to him the way she did when she found out. She was right in his face, demanding answers."

Travis shifted the sleeping toddler slightly, his gaze fixed on Nathaniel. "What I want to know is what brought on this epiphany? And how did you come to witness it?"

Yeah. Nathaniel had hoped not to go there. On the other hand, the time for secrets was past if they wanted to move forward. He, for one, definitely wanted to get past this.

"Ainsley's mother worked for Jason during that time period. She probably knew all about it and hoped to benefit from it herself."

"Wait, what?" Adam rubbed his forehead. "Ainsley's mother was involved with Uncle Jason? Isn't that about the time of his divorce from Aunt Ellen?"

"Yeah, I think so. Ainsley has a half-sister who would have been conceived about that time. I suspect she's Jason's daughter, but I don't have any proof of that."

Noah surged to his feet and paced across to the kitchen before pivoting. "I'd hazard a very strong guess otherwise. I met Ainsley's sister last night when I went to pick up the twins from youth group. Our sisters clicked with Vivienne practically at first sight."

What was his twin getting at?

Noah looked from one brother to the next, starting with Travis and ending with Nathaniel. "Ainsley's sister looks an awful lot like Emma and Alexia. It may be coincidence but, on the other hand, it may not be."

The only sound in Nathaniel's cabin was a snuffly sigh from a sleepy toddler as she turned her head against Travis's chest.

CHAPTER SEVENTEEN

Pumping Hector for information was like sending a bucket down a dry well that had only a few damp pebbles in the bottom. No cool drink would be forthcoming. Either he'd promised Mom not to tell her secrets, or he didn't know much.

Ainsley suspected the latter. The man had always seemed to lack curiosity, counting on Mom to ferret out any information he needed. He'd lived in a simple, narrow world for the ten or fifteen years Ainsley had known him, seemingly content with the day-in, day-out world of his brother's plumbing business.

Hector shrugged a large shoulder. "That, there, is everything I have of your mother's. She put that lockbox I told you about inside. It has to be enough."

Ainsley looked at the small cardboard box in her hands. Her name was written on it with a Sharpie in Mom's tidy hand. "Thanks."

Hector nodded. "Take care then." He started to close the door.

That was it? All the phone calls had been just for one box, and Ainsley was no longer welcome in the home she'd spent her teen years? But everything had been his. She couldn't remember a stitch of furniture or much of anything her mother had brought into their relationship. Mom hadn't been one to cling to the past.

Ainsley took a deep breath. "Bye, Hector."

He nodded and closed the door the rest of the way.

She retraced her steps to her car then slid inside and looked back at the small, unassuming house. She'd dropped her sister off at Stacy's when they'd arrived in the city. Turned out to be a good thing they'd packed Vivienne's clothes and trinkets and left most of them at Stacy's before driving to Jewel Lake a few weeks back.

Ainsley didn't want to sit in front of Hector's house while she looked through what her mom had left her, but where could she go?

The cemetery. It only took a few minutes to find Mom's grave.

Ainsley set down the box and the utility knife she'd pulled from her emergency bag then traced her mom's name and dates on the simple stone.

"Lord?" she whispered. "I miss my mom, but mostly I miss what could have been. I don't understand her choices, but I still loved her."

Her gaze slid back to the box. "I'm not sure I'm ready for this, whatever it is. What if there's nothing meaningful, and Vivienne and I never get any answers? Or what if…"

She rested her hand on the box and closed her eyes. "Jesus, please guide me and protect me from harm." Everything seemed so volatile since her memories had returned.

The headaches had lessened dramatically — a great side effect — and how could she not fall back in love with Nathaniel? Yet their parents' secrets had driven a wedge between them.

She'd run. She needed to stop running, but… "Lord, I'm afraid of Declan Cavanagh. How can I stay in Nathaniel's life and not run afoul of his stepfather?"

But God was her Father. He was bigger, bolder, *better* than Declan. If God was on her side, what could any man do to her? That was in Romans eight. Surely, it covered Declan. Besides, his two-year-old threat had already been exposed. She hadn't stuck around to find out if there was more.

Enough. She engaged the utility knife blade, cut the tape securing the cardboard box, and opened the flaps. At the top lay an envelope with her name on it. She stared at it for a long moment, then tucked it under her thigh. Inside the box were a few pieces of her mom's costume jewelry. A couple of scarves. An antique sugar bowl, now swathed in bubble wrap, that had once belonged to Grandma Johnson.

A ribbon held a dozen or so photos together, including a few of their little family. Bittersweet memories bubbled up. She'd make copies for Vivienne.

So few remnants of nearly fifty years of life. Tears coursed down Ainsley's cheeks. "Oh, Mom…"

At the bottom of the box lay the promised lockbox. And, yes, it was locked.

Finally, she used the knife to slit the envelope. A little key tumbled out, clinking on the gravestone. Ainsley carefully set it on top of the lockbox and pulled out the folded paper.

Dear Ainsley,

I know I'm dying. I need you to understand that everything I've done has been to protect you and your sister, since my mama taught me what you don't know can't hurt you. I'm not sure anymore if that's true. The more I think about my secrets, the more I suspect it's not. I know you have questions. I can't give you all the answers.

Ainsley stared out across the cemetery. Her mom couldn't or wouldn't? If only Ainsley hadn't lost her memories. If only she'd pushed her mom until she'd revealed the hidden things while she still could. Now she remained at Mom's mercy. Whatever her mother had decided to divulge was all Ainsley would ever get.

She blinked tears aside and refocused on the paper.

You've always wondered who your father was. I wish I could tell you, but I honestly don't know. I was a free spirit in my college days, partying and drinking too much. And then I was pregnant. I've tried to bring you up better than that. I didn't have much use for religion, but maybe it would have helped me then as it has you in recent years.

The paper trembled in Ainsley's hand.

No answers. No information about her birth father would ever be forthcoming. Ainsley couldn't very well track down every man who'd attended UW during her mom's four years to see if they might share her DNA. And the man might simply have crashed a party and not even been a student.

She would never know her father.

In that moment, she felt her heavenly Father's arms around her.

See what great love the Father has lavished on us, that we should be called children of God! And that is what we are!

God was enough. More than enough. Would He be for Vivienne, too?

Ainsley refocused on her mom's tidy handwriting.

Vivienne... well, I'm not proud of that period of my life. I worked for Jason Anderson in Jewel Lake. Maybe you already remembered that. He was not a good man, but decent jobs were hard to find, especially ones during school hours so I didn't need to hire a sitter for you.

When I discovered my boss was trying to fleece his own dying brother, I was horrified. Minutes after this revelation, an acquaintance came into the office to reassign his policy's beneficiary after a divorce. When he pressed me about my nervousness, I said too much. In my defense, my boss was attempting something potentially illegal.

Declan. It had to have been Declan Cavanagh.

Ainsley scanned the remainder quickly, but no names were named. Mom had become pregnant. The man had convinced her to leave town. Promised child support if she'd keep quiet, since he was remarrying...

Everything pointed to Nathaniel's stepfather. That uncanny resemblance between Emma, Alexia, and Vivienne was not a fluke of nature. The girls were half-sisters.

Ainsley's head spun, like it so often had before she passed out during her time of amnesia. *Not today, Satan.* She needed to keep herself together. Needed to stay focused on her own true Father, God.

Needed to open the lockbox.

She inserted the little key into the slot with trembling hands. Turn. Click. The lid released to reveal more papers.

At the bottom lay two birth certificates. Ainsley's, with 'father unknown' typed in, and Vivienne's, with 'Declan Cavanagh' in the same spot.

Ainsley reeled. It was true.

No wonder the man had threatened Ainsley to leave their family alone. He'd probably thought she knew everything and had returned to blackmail him or something like that.

But she couldn't keep this secret under wraps. Not now, when she had evidence. Could she?

It wasn't fair to Vivienne. It wasn't fair to Nathaniel or any of his brothers. Or his sisters.

Ainsley riffled through the remaining papers, mostly bank statements showing regular automated deposits from a Wells Fargo account in Jewel Lake.

Declan had kept his word to support his illegitimate daughter. That was something, at least.

"SHE'S NOISY." Travis's five-year-old son, Toby, looked up at Nathaniel with a frown. "Why is she screaming?"

Nathaniel sighed. "She wants her mama."

Toby nodded wisely. "Mamas are good."

Wasn't that the truth? Nathaniel unbuckled Bella from her car seat and hoisted her to his hip. At least the crying lessened. How could a kid possibly cry for two days? He would never have thought it possible. He'd planned to drive to town after Ainsley called that she and her sister had reached Missoula, but he couldn't wait. Couldn't wait to see her. Couldn't wait to hand off the distraught child.

He eyed his nephew. "Do you want to play with Bella? Maybe you can make her happy. Her mama will be here soon."

Toby angled his head and studied Bella. "Does she like horses?"

Nathaniel grinned at the reminder of Toby's cowboy-themed bedroom and the boy's equal love for his pony, Clover, up at the ranch. "She doesn't know much about them yet. But she might chew on your toy horses, so maybe try the blocks or something like that."

"Okay." Toby patted Bella's foot and looked up at her. "Come play with me, Bella, but don't cry. Your mama is coming."

Nathaniel ruffled the boy's hair. "You're a good kid, you know that?"

"I know."

With a chuckle, Nathaniel beeped the truck locks and followed Toby inside Travis and Dakota's rental.

Dakota met them at the door, arms outstretched for Bella. "Oh, she's beautiful, Nathaniel. Congratulations. I can't wait to meet Ainsley."

Should he be praised for getting his girlfriend pregnant? It didn't feel like something he should be commended for. On the other hand, God's grace and forgiveness covered it all.

Dakota lifted Bella over her head, jiggling her and talking baby talk. Bella grinned and babbled back.

Seriously. Why couldn't Nathaniel get that kind of response from his child? He'd bitten off way more than he could chew with a two-day visit so early in their relationship.

"Mama?" Toby tugged at his mom's top. "Bella's here to play with me, not you."

"Sorry, buddy." Dakota squatted beside her son and set Bella down between her knees. "Babies put everything in their mouths, so we need to be really careful what she can reach, okay?"

"Unca Nat said she might eat my horses!"

"Oh, no! Better keep your bedroom door closed then. What would she like to play with, do you think?"

"Blocks." Toby nodded assertively. "I'll go get them. You take care of her for a minute, okay, Mama?"

"Okay."

Toby dashed off, and Dakota looked up at Nathaniel. "Travis said it's been a little rough this weekend?"

"You could say that." He hesitated. "How do I know I'm cut out to be a father?"

"You're seriously asking that? She's, what, a year and a half old?"

"Sixteen months."

"It doesn't matter if you're 'cut out' to be a dad or not, Nat. You *are* one. No one gets a manual. You figure it out as you go. Ask God for wisdom. Do your best."

"She probably hates me after this weekend."

"It will be fine. Trust me. Just keep being there for her, day in and day out."

Across the space, Toby dumped out a bin of brightly colored wooden blocks. "Bella! Come play with me!"

The little girl pushed against Dakota's loose hold and toddled over, babbling. Not crying. Chalk one up for Toby and his mom. Bella chortled as she knocked over the small stack Toby made.

Nathaniel dared relax for the first time since yesterday morning. "Where's Trav?"

"He and Blake went for a hike after church, but they should be home any minute."

A not-surly Travis who cared about others was still a shock to Nathaniel's system.

Dakota turned into the kitchen. "They'll be coming back starving. Have you eaten recently, Nathaniel?"

He'd skipped church and lunch out at the Golden Grill with his family, thanks to an inconsolable toddler, so his schedule was off. "I had crackers and cheese a while back." Hadn't he?

"Men," muttered Dakota. "Fix yourself a sandwich while Bella's distracted. Or is she hungry, too?"

Nathaniel straightened his shoulders. "I've given her everything Ainsley sent, right on the suggested schedule."

"That's a start." Dakota pointed at the fridge. "There's ham and chicken in there. Help yourself. I'm going to finish making a potato salad to go with dinner. Do you want to stay? I think Blake is."

"I—"

"Trav's grilling steaks."

"Uh, sure. Probably?" Sundays were Cook's day off, so everyone at Rockstead fended for themselves anyway.

His phone pinged with an incoming text, and his heart lurched.

Ainsley: *In Missoula.*

Was it better to meet her again in front of others, or should he go over to her place? A quick glance in the living room where Bella chortled at Toby's comic faces settled that question. He texted back with Travis and Dakota's address and asked Ainsley to come by.

But now he was nervous. They'd left things horribly the last few times they'd seen each other. He loved her. That hadn't changed. But he couldn't trust her not to run out on him.

Couldn't trust her not to be like her mother, sabotaging other people's lives for money. And, if Noah was right, sleeping around to either cover up what she was doing or to get more information.

But Ainsley hadn't slept with Nathaniel for either of those reasons. She wasn't her mother. They'd shared something beautiful, and the result had been an adorable toddler. Adorable now that she wasn't sobbing inconsolably in his ear, anyway.

How could he separate Ainsley from the havoc her mother had wreaked in the lives of the Andersons and possibly the Cavanaghs?

No. He needed time to find out the truth. To sort out what it all meant to him.

That God loved no matter what wasn't lost on him. But he wasn't God. He was only human.

CHAPTER EIGHTEEN

T hat must be the place." Vivienne pointed out the duplex down the block with three Rockstead Ranch pickups in front. "I wonder if Alexia and Emma are here. That's their brother's house, right?"

Ainsley took a deep breath. So much for having a quiet conversation with Nathaniel. She had some apologizing to do — along with some revelations — but not in front of half the Cavanagh family. "I guess we'll see."

Mere weeks ago, this uncertainty and fear would have been enough to trigger one of those fearful headaches that sometimes culminated in blacking out. It was a good sign that those had lessened, for sure, but it also meant she had to deal with her fears head on.

"I can't wait to see Bella!" Vivienne's hand hovered over the door handle as Ainsley pulled to a stop behind one of the trucks.

"Me, too." Ainsley hadn't told her sister anything on the drive beyond they'd talk later. Thankfully Vivienne had let it go, alternating between telling Ainsley the news Stacy had shared about their mutual friends and excitement at getting to go horseback riding at Rockstead with her new ones. She seemed content with Ainsley holding information for later.

How much later? It remained to be seen, but she needed to talk to Nathaniel first. They'd plan a course of action together.

After that… would they actually *be* together? Or would Bella go back and forth between them like Dakota and Travis had shared Toby for four years? Not everyone had a happy ending like that little family. But she could still pray it would happen when all this mess was over.

Ainsley walked up the short sidewalk beside her sister then pressed the doorbell.

Toby flung the door open. "Bella's mama is here. Come see, Bella!"

No screaming. That was a good start. Nathaniel had done okay. The tension in Ainsley's spirit tapered just a little.

She stepped inside and crouched as her beautiful daughter trundled toward her, nearly tripping over her own tiny feet. "Mama, mama, mama!"

Ainsley clutched Bella to her chest and stood. "Oh, Bella Babe. Mama's missed you so, so much." She closed her eyes and soaked in the smell of baby and the feel of pudgy arms scrunching her neck.

When she opened them again, three cowboys stood in a ring staring at her, a tall, slender woman with them. She focused on Nathaniel. "Hi."

"Hey. I hope you had a good trip." His fists flexed at his sides.

She longed to throw herself into his arms, but she wouldn't assume that. Not in front of his brothers. She glanced between the others. "I'm Ainsley, but I guess you figured that out."

The guy who looked like a younger version of Declan Cavanagh gave a slight grin. "I'm Travis. This is my wife, Dakota, and my kid brother Blake." He nodded toward Vivienne, eyeing her speculatively. "And you must be Vivienne. Come on in."

He couldn't have guessed, could he? Maybe. But Ainsley shook her head. "I just need to gather Bella's things and get home. It's been a long two days."

Dakota stepped forward. "It's five o'clock, and dinner's almost ready here. There's plenty, and we'd love to get to know you better. I mean, I'm sure you're tired from your trip, but this way you wouldn't have to cook the minute you get home."

"That's very nice of you, but…" But what? Dakota was right. Ainsley would likely have to get takeout, and her budget was stretched thin enough as it was with this trip back to Spokane. She glanced at Vivienne, who offered a wide-eyed look, then turned back to Dakota. "If you're sure."

"Absolutely. Trav, throw on a couple of extra steaks, okay?"

He nuzzled her hair. "Your wish is my command, love."

Blake stuck his finger in his mouth in a gagging motion.

Vivienne giggled.

Dakota shook her head, but she was smiling. "Into the kitchen, Blake. I can put you to work, too. Come on in, Vivienne."

The woman was smooth. Everyone scattered, even little Toby, leaving Ainsley clutching Bella and facing Nathaniel.

"How was your trip?" His face was unreadable.

She'd caused that. "It was okay. Interesting."

One eyebrow tilted up just a smidge. "Anything you want to share?"

Bella grabbed Ainsley's face between two chubby hands and peered straight into her eyes from three inches away. "Mama."

"Yes, baby girl. Mama's here. Were you a good girl for Daddy?"

Nathaniel snorted.

Okay. Maybe not, then. Ainsley took as deep a breath as she could with both cheeks squished in. "We need to talk, but not right now."

"Did you get answers?" His voice was quiet.

"Some, yes. Not all." She managed to focus on him past Bella's curls. "It didn't go so well here, then?"

He hesitated, like he was afraid to tell her the truth. "She really missed you," he said at last.

"She's just a baby, and she'd never been apart from me before."

"Right. Well, we survived."

Voices and laughter came from the kitchen just around the corner, reminding Ainsley not to probe too deeply at the moment.

Nathaniel sidled a little closer. "I missed you, too. Not just because Bella did."

"I missed you, too." It seemed he'd gotten past what her mother had been part of with his uncle. Too bad Mom's story was even more entwined with Nathaniel's than he suspected. The revelations weren't over by a long shot.

She couldn't keep Vivienne's parentage from her much longer. That wasn't right, not at all. But exposing that history was going to affect Nathaniel's entire fractured family.

What would they have left at the other end of it?

NATHANIEL SAT on Ainsley's sofa, hands clasped and head bowed. From upstairs, he could hear Vivienne's music pulse quietly and the rocking chair creak as Ainsley settled their daughter for bed.

A heavy question nagged at him. Was he going to tell Ainsley Noah's suspicion about Vivienne's parentage? Was it slander to put Declan's name forward in that scenario? Nathaniel didn't have any evidence. Confronting his step-father without proof wasn't wise or helpful. Maybe it was just as wrong to mention it to Ainsley.

It was idle speculation based on Noah's hunch. Nothing more. But what if it was the clue Ainsley needed to figure out the past?

Nathaniel lurched to his feet and crossed to the window. A gentle summer rain pattered against the pane and streaked the dust on his pickup in the driveway. The verdant view of plump grass and riotous flowers filled the foreground, but there was a glimpse of Miner's Rock across the lake between the two rooflines across the street.

I lift my eyes to the mountains — where does my help come

from? My help comes from the Lord, the Maker of heaven and earth.

No amount of worrying was going to solve this problem. God had it all under control. However, there were no promises Nathaniel would like the outcome.

Psalm 37 came to mind, and he thumbed open the Bible app on his phone and read it. *Trust in the Lord and do good; dwell in the land and enjoy safe pasture. Take delight in the Lord, and he will give you the desires of your heart. Commit your way to the Lord; trust in him and he will do this: he will make your righteous reward shine like the dawn, your vindication like the noonday sun. Be still before the Lord and wait patiently for him...*

Nathaniel wasn't sure he deserved a righteous reward, never mind vindication, but the rest of it felt like a whisper from the Almighty.

Ainsley's footsteps descended the staircase, and he turned toward her. She was so gorgeous, even in capri-length jeans and a simple T-shirt. She'd bundled her hair into a low bun.

He wanted to kiss that exposed neck, but this wasn't the time. They'd exchanged heated words a few days back, and the atmosphere had been tight when he'd picked up Bella yesterday morning. No way was Ainsley coming up to the ranch any time soon. Not after the debacle with Declan. Nathaniel could hardly blame her for that.

Was there really any hope for them?

Nathaniel tried to push the negative thought out of his mind. *Commit your way to the Lord; trust in him...Be still before the Lord and wait patiently for him.*

Patiently. But hopefully not too long.

She went over to the table, where she'd set a cardboard box when they'd come over from Travis and Dakota's. She opened the flaps slowly, then looked at him across the space before lifting out a blue lockbox. "There are some things in here I think you need to see."

Nathaniel tried to keep the surprise from showing. "Okay." He crossed the space and stood around the corner of the table from her. "What is it?"

She glanced toward the staircase. "Vivienne's original birth certificate."

Ainsley's voice was so low he strained to hear her. His heart thumped madly. Suddenly, he didn't want to know the answer to the puzzle. He didn't want the brothers' speculation to be right.

Maybe it wasn't. Maybe Vivienne's father was... Pastor Smith. Well, that was highly unlikely, but just because Ainsley was so serious didn't mean it was Declan. Did it?

She unlocked the box with a small key and tilted the open lid toward him.

A birth certificate lay on top. Vivienne Joan Johnson. Mother: Brenda Marie Johnson. Father: Declan Cavanagh.

Nathaniel's knees weakened and he clenched the back of the chair in front of him. "No way," he whispered.

"I know it must be a big shock," Ainsley said quietly then bit down on her bottom lip.

He took a deep breath. "Not as much as you might think."

"What do you mean?"

"Noah mentioned... he was struck by how much Vivienne looks like Alexia and Emma. It was sheer speculation on his part, though." The admission seemed like nothing compared to the reality.

Ainsley let out her breath in a whoosh. "I saw the same thing Friday night. I guess that niggle prepared me for seeing the reality in black and white on legal paperwork. And my mom left me a letter, which corroborates the birth certificate."

"What did she say? Not that it's any of my business. Sorry. I shouldn't have asked."

Wordlessly, she passed over a folded piece of paper.

Nathaniel searched her face before smoothing the paper out and scanning the contents. Ainsley's own paternity questions remained unanswered, but there was at least a little detail about what had happened with Jason and Declan back then. And Brenda's words seemed to exonerate her in the matter of the Anderson inheritance.

He looked back at Ainsley. "I'm sorry."

Tears welled in her blue eyes. "Me, too."

Nathaniel reached for her hand. "Can we get past this? Please?"

"I don't know how you can say that. My mother…"

"Your mother isn't you, sweetheart. She made some poor choices, but she also made some good ones."

"But… Declan."

"I know." And it all needed to come into the open. If the other day hadn't pounded the final nail in the coffin of Mom and Declan's marriage, this surely would. But truth still needed to be spoken. Gently. In love.

"I don't want him to be her father! He threatened me. He scares the living daylights out of me. He's not ever going to be the daddy she's always dreamed of. She's better off without him."

"I don't think this can be hidden. Or should be."

"Maybe Vivienne is better off not knowing." Ainsley refolded the letter and set it in the top of the lockbox.

"It doesn't change the facts."

"Better off not knowing what?"

Nathaniel pivoted at hearing Vivienne's voice right behind him. Oh, boy. Nothing like controlling how information escaped.

"Nothing." Ainsley slapped the lockbox lid down and reached for the key, but it slipped from her hands and bounced on the floor.

Before Nathaniel could react, Vivienne dove under the table and came up with the object. She held it up by her face with one hand and held out the other for the lockbox. "Please pass that over here." Her voice was crisp. Hard.

"Vivi, you don't want—"

"Right now, Ainsley."

"Please don't…"

But when Vivienne didn't relent, Ainsley stepped back and burst into tears. Both hands came up to her face and covered it. Sobs wracked her body.

Nathaniel couldn't stand it. Let Vivienne make what she would of the letter and birth certificate. It didn't need any extra explanation. His job was Ainsley, who'd run up the stairs.

He maybe shouldn't go up there, but he had to. She needed him, whether she knew it or not. Nathaniel took the steps two at a time, only pausing when Vivienne uttered a guttural scream.

Ainsley's bedroom door clicked shut in his face, and he knocked on it. "Ainsley, sweetheart, let me in."

From her bedroom, Bella gave a startled cry.

Nathaniel tried the knob, but Ainsley had locked the door. Now what? Three females, all of them royally upset. *Lord? I could use some help here.*

CHAPTER NINETEEN

Ainsley tumbled onto her bed and curled into a fetal ball. No, no, no.

From downstairs, Vivienne yelled, "Ainsley, you come back here right now!"

Nathaniel knocked on her door. "Ainsley? Please let me in." His voice was quiet but firm.

Bella wailed from her room next door.

Footsteps pounded on the stairs, and Vivienne's voice became louder. "Ainsley! Why didn't you tell me?" Fists battered the door.

Why couldn't she run? Just climb out the window and never come back? But the three people she loved most in this world were on the other side of her bedroom door, all of them needing her, at least one of them furiously angry.

Be still, and know that I am God.

The psalmist's words settled in Ainsley's mind. Running didn't work. God knew she'd done enough of that. It was time to stop running, stop hiding, and start facing things.

She rubbed tears from her cheeks as she stumbled to the door and opened it.

Only Vivienne stood there, her eyes red and her face blotchy. Down the hallway, Nathaniel murmured to Bella, who still sobbed.

Vivienne held up the paper. "Is this true?"

Ainsley swallowed hard. "There's no reason to believe it is *not* true. The birth certificate is a legal document, and the bank statements corroborate it."

"Bank statements?"

"They're in the lockbox, too."

Vivienne took a few steps away then pivoted back and wrapped her arms around Ainsley. "Oh, sis. What does this really mean?"

"It doesn't matter. We're sisters. Always and forever here for each other."

"But the twins…"

"Are equally your sisters." Oh, how it pained her to say those words.

"Not equally." Vivienne squeezed tighter. "You've been there for me every minute of my life."

"Thanks." Tears threatened to burst the fountain open again.

"Is my father a good man?" whispered Vivienne. "Do you know him?"

"He's… challenging. I've only met him a couple of times. This is going to be very difficult for the whole Cavanagh family."

Vivienne pushed to arms-length. "Does this mean I'm related to Nathaniel? Because that's just weird."

"It would be." Ainsley managed a smile. "But, no. He and

Emma and Alexia share a mother. You and the twins share a father. There's no blood relationship between you and Nathaniel."

"Whew."

"You can say that again."

"Mama!"

Ainsley looked past Vivienne to see Nathaniel holding Bella, who held her hands out to her.

"Sorry." He looked apologetic. "I picked her up. I'm not sure if you would have left her to fall back asleep on her own."

"It's fine." Ainsley held Bella close, and the toddler tucked her sweaty, tousled head into the crook of her mama's shoulder and slurped her thumb into her mouth.

Nathaniel looked at Vivienne. "Welcome to the family? Don't worry. We'll get everything sorted out."

Vivienne lifted the birth certificate. "Looks sorted to me."

"I know." He offered a half-smile. "People are more complicated than papers. But we won't make you navigate this by yourself."

"Thanks." Vivienne flung herself into Nathaniel's arms. "This is exciting… and totally terrifying."

He patted her back awkwardly and looked past her to Ainsley. "You're right on both counts. But we'll do it together. All of us. I promise."

"Okay." Vivienne sniffled. "I'm kind of scared."

Bella drooped against Ainsley's shoulder, her eyes blinking shut.

"You two go downstairs. I'll lay her down and be there right away."

Nathaniel searched Ainsley's face for a minute then nodded. "C'mon, Viv." Keeping his arm draped over Vivienne's shoulder, he led her to the stairs.

Ainsley sagged into the rocking chair and snuggled her toddler until the little body was limp against her. This was almost enough time to gather her thoughts and emotions into something controllable. Almost, but not quite.

All she could do was plead with Jesus to keep guiding them and to help Declan come to grips with the fact his indiscretion was public without blaming her. But how would it come out? Would Ainsley and Vivienne have to stand in front of him and tell him the gig was up?

No. Nathaniel had said he'd be there, right beside them.

She loved that cowboy. She really did. She didn't deserve his forgiveness or his favor, yet he continued to offer it. Considering all that had gone down, he was letting her off more easily than she deserved.

Like God. Ainsley didn't deserve the good gifts He had given her, either, but still He loved her and comforted her and forgave her.

With a deep exhale, she laid Bella back in her crib, tiptoed out of the room, and made her way downstairs to where Vivienne and Nathaniel had spread the meager contents of the box out on the kitchen table.

So few pieces remained of her mom's life. But Ainsley and Vivienne and even Bella were Brenda Johnson's legacy. They could make it a good one.

Ainsley straightened her shoulders.

WHEW. Those few minutes had done Ainsley a world of good. She held her head high and her back straight, while a tremulous smile hovered on her face.

Nathaniel felt the tension ease out of him as he met her gaze. "You okay?"

"As okay as I'm going to be right now, under the circumstances."

Fair enough. He shifted closer and held out his arms. Would she accept his comfort after all that had happened in the past few days?

Ainsley searched his face then stepped into his embrace. Her arms went around his middle as she leaned against his chest.

He held her close and rested his cheek against her hair. This was where she belonged. They had to get past this — through this — whatever it took, so they could refocus on being a family. They already were one, but still fractured.

Vivienne unwound the bubble-wrap from around a package Nathaniel had noticed in the box. She held up an old sugar bowl with painted flowers on the side, but the handles were missing.

"That was Grandma Johnson's. Do you remember her? She died when you were little."

Vivienne shook her head. "It's pretty, even though it's broken."

Ainsley pushed out of Nathaniel's arms. "Mom tucked the arms inside it. I don't remember when it broke, though."

Vivienne looked between him and her sister. "What are we going to do?"

Ainsley hugged her sister. "I don't know, but we will definitely do something."

Nathaniel cleared his throat. "May we start by getting my brothers together, and we can tell them everything? Show them the papers. We had a meeting Saturday night, and Noah mentioned that he thought you really resembled Alexia and Emma."

"He did? I do?" Vivienne touched her face.

"I saw it, too. But I wasn't sure until all this." Ainsley pointed to the objects spread across the table. "It could have been coincidence or my over-active imagination."

Vivienne stared at Nathaniel. "I have brothers, too."

"You do. Travis and Blake and Ryder are your half-brothers."

The teen sank onto one of the chairs beside the table. "This is huge."

"As I was saying, I'd like to get my brothers together. Declan's sons and my full brothers. I think the five of them need to know first. Then my mom and the twins. And then we'll figure out how to bring it up with Declan. Together."

Nathaniel's mind raced through the possibilities of how his mother and Declan would react. While Vivienne's conception had been before Declan's marriage to Mom, he'd known all these years, and Nathaniel was pretty sure his mother had no clue. But then, she might not have confided in any of her sons. Adam had been barely a teen when all this went down.

Ainsley pressed her hand to her heart. "When?"

"It's too late tonight. Blake might still be at Travis and Dakota's, but cell signal is too weak at the ranch to get in touch with Adam or Ryder. I could probably get Noah.

He's shoeing horses around Seeley Lake for a couple of days."

"I-I don't want to go back to Rockstead to confront Declan." Ainsley's voice shook, but her chin was up.

"I agree. Best to get him off his home turf." He hesitated. "Can I see if Travis is willing to host us and my brothers Tuesday evening? Then we can make plans for the next stage."

"Will my father be angry about me?" Vivienne sounded wistful.

"He has a temper, for sure." There wasn't any point trying to sugarcoat Declan Cavanagh to his newest daughter. "It's hard to know exactly how he'll react. Are you sure you want to go through with this? We can keep the secret between us, if you want. It's up to the two of you."

A long look passed between Vivienne and Ainsley.

"Look, I'm gonna walk around the block a couple of times. Call me when you've had a chance to talk." Nathaniel grabbed his cowboy hat from the rack by the door and exited the house before one of the women could tell him it wasn't necessary. It was. He wasn't part of their household.

Man, he hated walking, but Kingpin was up at Rockstead. Still, either riding or walking gave him the chance to talk to God, and he had a funny feeling that he was going to need God's guidance more than ever before.

They were sitting on a powder keg.

If Vivienne decided against setting off the fuse, it would still blow at some point. Best to do it while they could sort of control the timing of the explosion.

But Declan could go rogue, no matter when or how this happened.

Prayer was a requirement.

THE DOOR CLICKED SHUT behind Nathaniel, and Ainsley turned to her sister. "He's right. It's up to you. If you want, we can pack this paperwork away and pretend we never saw it." Which would mean leaving Jewel Lake and Nathaniel behind. Could her heart take that decision?

"You're delusional." Vivienne rolled her eyes. "How good an actor do you think you are? I'm terrible. I went stiff like a robot in drama tryouts, which is why I've never gotten a part in the school play yet."

Ainsley managed a smile. "I'm pretty bad, too. But the point remains. Once this comes out, we can't control the fallout."

"Ains, I love you. You know that. But I just found out the two cool kids I met a few days ago are my sisters, too. And I have three brothers." A look of wonder crossed her face. "And that cute Toby kid is actually my nephew?"

Was Ainsley losing her sister already? She wrapped her arms around her middle. She'd never find the other half of her family, not unless some middle-aged man showed up with a DNA test in tow to claim her. That wasn't going to happen. Mom's letter had pretty much slammed the door on those daydreams.

All her family was in this house. Her half-sister, Vivienne. Her daughter, Bella. There would never be anyone more.

But Nathaniel was here for her. He wanted to marry her. She could be part of the Cavanagh family, too, and close her family's circle. If Nathaniel even still wanted her when all this had blown over.

"Ainsley?"

She blinked away the tears that had formed while she processed the whole family thing. "I'm happy for you, Viv. I mean it. I think we should take Nathaniel up on his idea and meet with all his brothers. What do you think?"

"I want to. Emma and Alexia are awesome, and Travis and Blake seem like nice guys. They won't let anything bad happen to me, will they?"

"They won't. They absolutely won't. They'll build a wall around you, six cowboys strong, if it's needed."

"Is God... is God gonna help?"

"Oh, sweetie." Ainsley hugged her sister. "He absolutely will be your strength and shield."

"Let's do it. I'm gonna go find Nathaniel." Vivienne strode over to the door then turned with her hand on the knob. "He's a keeper, Ainsley. Don't let him get away."

She wouldn't. Not if she could help it. Not if he'd have her.

CHAPTER TWENTY

Blake draped his arm over Nathaniel's shoulder and waved a can of pop at the other brothers standing around Travis and Dakota's home. "I'm sure you're wondering why I've called you all together like this." He patted Nathaniel. "That was your line, dude. Take it away."

It was Wednesday evening, since Noah'd been working out of town and couldn't get back sooner.

Now that the moment was here, Nathaniel's words had dried up. This disclosure was going to change their family forever, just as momentous as when their parents had married seventeen years ago, and Declan had claimed the Anderson boys as his legal sons.

"Is this an engagement announcement?" Riley, Adam's wife, glanced between him and Ainsley with an expectant smile.

Ainsley drew back a step, and Riley's bright eyes dimmed.

"Not today, no." It was coming, or so Nathaniel hoped, but this was a barrier that needed to be hurdled before his personal happiness. He drew in a deep breath as he put an arm across Vivienne's shoulder. "I'd like you all to meet Ainsley's seventeen-year-old sister, Vivienne."

Dakota's brows drew together as she and Travis exchanged a puzzled glance.

"She's Declan's daughter."

The fuse had been ignited, and it only took two seconds for the stunned silence to blow apart in an explosion of disbelief and questions.

Noah nodded from across the room.

He'd suspected all along. Even though he'd voiced it at their last brotherly meeting, it seemed the other four hadn't considered it a real possibility.

Nathaniel held up his hand, and the guys settled down. "Declan's name is on Vivienne's birth certificate, which Ainsley discovered last weekend in a box her mother left her. There are also automatic transfers from Declan's bank account — I confirmed the account numbers yesterday — to Brenda Johnson's account in Spokane for all these years."

Holding her mother's letter, Ainsley stepped up to Vivienne's other side. "We'll show you those things. Don't worry about that. But this is what my mother had to say about it all."

The paper quivered. Nathaniel wished he could support Ainsley in this difficult moment, but they'd agreed this was Vivienne's moment.

Ainsley read the entire letter, her voice growing stronger as she went.

She hadn't told him she was going to reveal her own dashed hopes of finding her father, but perhaps it was just as well to have everything in the open.

Ryder offered an incredulous laugh. "You're my sister?" He pried Vivienne out from between Nathaniel and Ainsley and twirled her. "This is crazy stuff."

Nathaniel closed the gap and clasped Ainsley's hand in his as the brothers gathered around Vivienne. "You're brave," he whispered.

"Because you're here," she whispered back, looking up at him.

"I'll always be here, if you'll let me." He lifted his free hand and brushed the side of her cheek.

From down the short hallway, Bella shrieked, her glee slicing the tumult in the living room.

"Use your inside voice!" commanded Toby.

Dakota laughed. "I'll check on them." She looked between Nathaniel and Ainsley and hurried to Toby's room.

Travis took his turn hugging Vivienne. "I'm sorry for what my dad did, but I'm thankful we found you. Not gonna lie, it's going to be a bit unpleasant around Rockstead for a bit, but then it will settle down. We'll make sure you're okay. We're Cavanagh strong."

"Cavanagh strong," echoed several of the brothers, Andersons included.

A little of the tension seeped out of Nathaniel. He'd known he could trust these guys, but now he *knew*. Things had sure changed between them all in the past couple of years since Adam had returned from the rodeo and Travis had gotten his head screwed on straight with Dakota and

Toby. Probably the younger guys also had issues, but for the first time since Nathaniel could remember, they were actually united on something. They were going to need to be, because the next step was the reveal to their parents and sisters. Their other sisters.

He gave his head a shake.

"Where do we go from here?" Adam asked from beside him.

"I think Mom needs to know."

"Declan's gonna go ballistic."

"Yeah." Nathaniel grimaced. "That's why I think Mom needs a heads-up."

"How about the twins?" Adam wanted to know.

"After Mom? And maybe before Declan."

"By like five minutes max. They can't keep a secret worth anything."

"True." Nathaniel considered the situation then shook his head. "We don't have the luxury of putting this off indefinitely, though."

"I agree." Travis had joined them. "It's Toby's birthday next week. Normally we'd have the party at Rockstead, but maybe, under the circumstances, we should have it here on Sunday afternoon."

"Could get ugly for the neighbors," Adam put in mildly.

Travis shrugged. "Sage Mulligan lives next door. She'd be cool with whatever."

"Adam's right," said Nathaniel. "Declan could impact a wider circle than the other half of this duplex."

"I still think we're better off here rather than up at the ranch. Dad will think twice about his reactions in town. He's got a reputation to uphold."

Adam snorted. "Everyone knows he's a hothead."

"But he's fair." Travis leveled a look at Adam. "He paid child support all these years, plus he's always treated you three the same as his own sons."

"Not sure I'd agree with that." Adam's hands fisted at his sides.

Nathaniel stepped between them. "Doesn't matter. We're talking about Vivienne here, not old stuff we've all forgiven each other for. Right?"

"Yeah." Adam relaxed his stance.

"You're right, Nat." Travis glared at Adam for a few more seconds before shaking his head. "Does anyone have a better idea than having it here? I'll admit I don't really want to ruin Toby's birthday, but I'm not sure how else to guarantee Dad will come to town when asked."

"And not too public, so not the gymkhana this weekend." Blake had sidled up beside them.

"Let's just do it on Sunday and not tie it to Toby's birthday," Nathaniel suggested. "I think Declan will come if you specifically ask him to, Travis. Do we tell Mom much in advance?"

The guys looked at each other.

Noah met Nathaniel's gaze. "They always come into town Sunday morning. Declan will drop Mom and the girls off at church, then he'll go for coffee with the guys at the Golden Grill. I think we should intercept Mom right after the twins go to youth class and bring her over here to Trav's place. One of us can go back for the twins after their class. And then just wait here until Declan comes to pick them up."

Blake's eyebrows rose. "And ambush him?"

Noah glanced at Blake. "Got a better idea? We're all ears."

The other guy lifted his hands and let them fall.

Guess not, then. Nathaniel eyed each brother in turn, realizing Ryder wasn't in their huddle. A quick glance to the rest of the group showed Ryder talking to Vivienne while Ainsley and Riley chatted nearby. Dakota must still be in the back with the younger generation. "I think Noah's got the best plan. I hate waiting that many days, but it's important to have a plan, and this is probably the best way to handle it."

"I wish we didn't have to skip church to do it." Noah sighed. "But it's just once."

Blake nodded. "You can get Pastor Marshall's sermon online later."

"I guess. It's not the same, though."

"So… is everyone agreed, then?" Nathaniel looked between the brothers.

They all put their hands into the middle. "Cavanagh strong."

"Three and a half days?" Vivienne looked at Ainsley in disbelief. "I wanted to go to youth group again on Friday."

"You still can."

Vivienne rolled her eyes. "There's no way I can hang out with Emma and Alexia and not say anything. I'm just bursting."

"I'm sorry it will take that long." Ainsley looked over at

Nathaniel as he came out of Travis and Dakota's place carrying Bella. "And I know you're here for only a few more weeks, so you'll want to spend every minute you can with them."

"We were going to go riding on Saturday. I suppose I can't do that, either."

Ainsley shuddered. "Probably wiser not to."

Nathaniel draped an arm over Vivienne's shoulder. "Next week. I'll see if you can come for the whole weekend."

"I guess it depends on how things go with my *dear papa*." Sarcasm laced the teen's words.

"There's that." Nathaniel met Ainsley's gaze. "Ready to go?"

The letdown was real. "I guess."

"I'm not abandoning you. Unless you want me to go back to the ranch already."

"Can you stay a little while?" Ainsley hated how needy she was, but everything had been such a whirlwind the past week, and they'd barely had five minutes to themselves.

"So… what if I *don't* go?"

It took Ainsley a few seconds to realize what Vivienne had said. "What do you mean?"

"Back to Spokane. I didn't know I had a family here when I made that plan. Besides you, I mean."

Ouch. Ainsley and Bella weren't enough to keep Vivienne, but Alexia and Emma were? And the brothers. Ainsley was going to have to get used to sharing her sister. Throwing this door open had changed all the dynamics she'd ever known.

Nathaniel squeezed Vivienne's shoulder before dropping his arm. "I'm pretty sure you'd be welcome to stay. Ainsley was really going to miss you."

"Of course." Jealousy still niggled, though. "It's time to get home and tuck Bella in bed. We can talk more about the possibilities."

Was it wrong that what she really wanted was for Vivienne to volunteer to take Bella upstairs so Ainsley could spend some time with Nathaniel? She didn't want to waste his time by rehashing all this over and over again. Not that she didn't want to be there for her kid sister. Of course, she did, but a little break from the drama would be welcome.

With a start she realized Nathaniel was already buckling Bella into her seat in his truck. Bella seemed to have gotten over her anger at being left with her daddy for two whole days last weekend.

Ainsley could take a page out of the toddler's book. Forgiveness was a thing. Moving forward was a thing. Not living in fear.

A few minutes later Nathaniel parked in Ainsley's driveway, and she pivoted in her seat. "Viv? Can I ask a favor?"

"Hmm?" Vivienne tucked her phone away. "What's up?"

"Would you please get Bella ready for bed?"

Vivienne's gaze ping-ponged between Ainsley and Nathaniel. "So you can smooch?"

Nathaniel chuckled. "I wouldn't say no to smooching."

Ainsley's cheeks warmed.

"Whatever." Vivienne rolled her eyes. "Yeah, fine, I've got Bella. But I'm still not happy about dragging this thing out so long."

It's not all about you. The retort died in Ainsley's mind. It might not *all* be about Vivienne, but a high percentage of it was. No doubt Declan's warning to Ainsley two years ago had been designed to keep her away from connecting the dots. Too late, buster. The dots had been fully connected, and he was on the hook for what he'd done.

"There's something else my brothers and I need to discuss," Nathaniel said as Vivienne carried Bella up the stairs a few minutes later.

Ainsley wanted to spend a few minutes forgetting the whole nasty mess existed. "What's that?"

"I think we need to have my uncle investigated. What if he actually managed to fleece some other families?"

Oh, no. Ainsley hadn't thought of that. "But… Carey."

"It's not on her, Ainsley. No more than Vivienne is to blame for Declan and your mom's tryst."

"I know, but it will crush her."

"Sometimes we have to do what's right, regardless."

Did they? Ainsley preferred pretending the world was a happy place. No wonder she'd struggled to overcome the amnesia. Her subconscious knew there was turmoil beneath the placid surface. Things she didn't want to deal with. Didn't have the tools for.

"My mom's letter made it sound like this thing with your parents was a one-time thing for Jason."

"Let's hope."

Ainsley laced her fingers with Nathaniel's. "This is all so scary. Thanks for sticking with Viv and me through it all."

His hand swept the side of her face. "I wouldn't be anywhere else. You have to know that you and Bella mean the world to me."

Her gaze caught on his. She opened her mouth to respond, but any words in her head fled before they could be uttered as his lips captured hers.

This. This was what coming home felt like.

CHAPTER TWENTY-ONE

Nathaniel nodded to Noah, and they stepped up on either side of their mother in the foyer of Creekside Fellowship.

"Hey, Mom."

She smiled at one then the other as she tucked her hands behind their elbows. "Have I told you recently how much it means to me to see my boys in church every week, knowing you are following after Jesus?"

Noah leaned in. "But we're playing hooky this week, and we're taking you with us."

Mom looked between them, her smile fading. "I've been looking forward to continuing with Pastor Marshall's series on forgiveness."

"We're planning to download the podcast later." Nathaniel nudged her toward the large windows next to the doors, wide open for the summer breeze.

"But…" She let go of their arms.

Twin-speak was useful. It only took a glance between the two of them to convey their plan.

It would have worked if not for Eli, the youth pastor. "Kathryn! Are the girls here today?"

"Yes, of course. They just went to class. How are you, Eli?"

"Doing well." Eli rocked back on his heels, his gaze taking in the three of them. "Sorry if I'm interrupting something."

If they weren't doing this during the worship hour, Nathaniel would invite Eli to come along. It was still a temptation, since the senior pastor, Marshall Smith, would be delivering the message. Eli knew the twins well. He'd be seeing the fallout of today's revelations soon.

Nathaniel shook his head ever so slightly at Noah's raised eyebrows. "We're kidnapping our mother. We've got something planned she needs to be a part of."

"Boys, really." Mom pushed them apart. "This is the Lord's day."

"Must be important," Eli said mildly.

"It is." Nathaniel and Noah spoke as one voice.

Eli tipped an imaginary hat and turned away.

"Come on, Mom."

She looked over her shoulder as they steered her toward the entrance. "But the girls. And where is your brother?"

"All taken care of. We're heading over to Trav's place. Eli hit the nail on the head. This really is important."

"Vitally so," Noah added as they exited the building. "Nat's truck is over here."

"Tell me what's going on."

"In a few minutes." Noah held the door for their mom as Nathaniel started the truck.

They kept the silence in the few minutes it took to pull up at the duplex. Whew. The other guys had parked around the back.

He opened the duplex door for his mom and Noah.

"Hey, Mom." That from Adam.

"Hi, Kathryn," chimed in Ryder and Blake.

Travis poured a cup of tea and extended it to Mom.

Mom pressed her hand to her chest. "All six of you? Okay, whatever it is, spill."

"Have a seat." Nathaniel pointed out the easy chair.

"You're scaring me." But she perched on the edge of the deep chair and set the teacup on the side table. "Okay. I'm ready."

"You met Ainsley the other day," Nathaniel began. "But when I brought her and Bella to the ranch, we left Ainsley's half-sister here in town. We didn't know she was an important part to the puzzle." Just imagine if they'd brought her then!

Mom's eyebrows tipped up slightly. "Puzzle?"

"As to why Declan decided to get involved with you and Running Creek."

"I don't understand."

"Ainsley's mom, Brenda, worked for Jason at the time. I suspected that she and Jason were very close. That Jason might be Vivienne's father, even."

Mom just looked at him, waiting. If she'd known about Vivienne previously, wouldn't there be some sort of reaction?

"It turns out that Ainsley's mother was horrified by what Jason was doing to you and to others. Or at least, what he was trying to do. We haven't yet figured out if he actually succeeded with anyone else."

Now she narrowed her gaze. "Go on."

"Declan was a client of Jason's. After his divorce, he made an appointment with Jason to get Monica's name removed from his life insurance policy. When he came to the office, Brenda had just uncovered some of Jason's duplicity."

Nathaniel swallowed hard. He didn't want to tell this story. Not again.

Travis picked up the tale. "One thing led to another, and Declan and Brenda had an affair that resulted in pregnancy. Ainsley's sister, Vivienne, is Declan's daughter."

Mom gasped, her hand covering her mouth as tears swelled in her eyes. "No. That can't be."

"His name is on her birth certificate." Travis set it on the table beside the teacup. "And there's further evidence he knew, because of the child support he paid every month for the past seventeen years."

"No. I don't understand."

Nathaniel knelt by his mother's chair and grasped her hand. "We've got the papers laid out on the kitchen table. There is really no doubt at all."

She cradled her head in her hands, leaning over her knees. "Oh, Lord Jesus, how do I bear this?"

"I don't know if it helps," Blake put in, "but it was before you married my dad."

"He lied to me."

Blake grimaced. "Yeah, that's probably true."

Adam stood behind Mom's chair and rubbed her back. "Mom, we'd like to introduce you to Vivienne. She's a cool kid, and she's already friends with Emma and Alexia from youth group. So, after the girls' teen class, Ryder is going to pick the two of them up. Then we'll tell them."

Mom shook her head. "You can't. This can't be public."

"It has to be, Mom," Adam said gently. "Think of a girl who's never belonged anywhere, who just found out she has two sisters and three brothers who are worth knowing, even if her father's a hotheaded jerk."

"Don't speak of Declan that way," Mom murmured.

Sticking up for her husband must be more out of habit than anything else. God knew the man didn't deserve Mom's loyalty.

Nathaniel glanced around at the guys from his position at his mother's knees. He received encouraging nods. "Then we want Declan to come here to pick you up, and we'll all tell him the gig is up."

She closed her eyes, swaying. Praying, no doubt. "Maybe this is the answer."

"The answer to what, Mom?" asked Noah quietly.

"Maybe... maybe I've had enough."

Nathaniel's heart bumped. "Of?"

"Of being controlled. Belittled. Unloved." She swiped at tears, and Noah plucked a tissue from a nearby box and handed it to her. "I love you boys. All of you." She looked between Travis and Blake and Ryder. "And your sisters. I never wanted to be the one who broke up a family."

Travis shifted closer. "You've been far more a mother to us than Monica ever was, for all she gave birth to us. We know..." He took a deep breath. "We understand how difficult Declan is. We wouldn't blame you if you made this decision. You'll always be our mom, regardless."

Mom stumbled to her feet and into Travis's arms. From there, she made her way between all six of them.

After Nathaniel's turn, he stood back, watching. Wishing Ainsley were here with him, but that would be soon enough. The women and kids were in the backyard, waiting to be summoned.

AINSLEY HAD NEVER BEEN with such a silent group of females. Even Vivienne had quieted after a few minutes of nervous babble, and Ainsley was pretty sure not much fazed Riley or Dakota.

Toby exhibited all kinds of patience with Bella in the sandbox.

Ainsley was primed to intervene, but there was no need. Not when Vivienne sat on the wooden edge and diverted toys as required.

Had Vivienne really meant that she might consider staying in Jewel Lake? It was hard to know what to think about that. Ainsley wanted to feel hurt that she and Bella hadn't been enough to make this shift on their own. But sharing Vivienne with the twins, with their brothers... so much was up in the air.

The truth hadn't set her free. It had entangled her feet like nothing in her life had before. Or maybe that wasn't quite true. The mess restraining her had always been there. She just hadn't been aware of it before, but now it was all so clear.

She wouldn't be surprised if Nathaniel backpedaled out of her life. Not that he'd given any indication he would, but how could he not? This revelation had blasted his entire family apart, and it was all Ainsley's fault.

If only she hadn't returned to Jewel Lake as an adult against Mom's expressed orders. Hadn't met Nathaniel and fallen for him and slept with him and gotten pregnant…

This spiral was almost a comfort place by now, so well-worn it was. But Bella was her anchor, and Nathaniel had forgiven her everything. He'd let her off easily from her running and deceit and everything.

Ainsley pushed against the spiral. It wasn't right. She knew it. Bella wasn't her anchor. Nathaniel wasn't, either. Jesus was. She needed to keep her eyes fixed on Him, not circumstances, not her worries and fears. She sent a prayer upward, then took a deep breath as the door opened and Nathaniel stepped out.

His gaze locked on hers in a loving caress that eased a little more of the tension. Then he turned to the teen. "Vivienne, it's time to meet my mom. Your stepmom. Are you ready?"

Vivienne bounced to her feet and dusted her hands down her denim shorts. "Yes. So ready."

Nathaniel's hand reached for Ainsley's. "Come, too?"

"I'll watch Bella," put in Dakota. "There will be enough family drama all day today. I don't need to witness every second of it."

Riley settled deeper into her deck chair. "Goes for me, too. We'll come inside in a bit."

Ainsley glanced at Bella, who dribbled a handful of sand over Toby's dump truck. "Okay." She let the warmth of Nathaniel's palm lend her comfort and strength as he ushered her and Vivienne into the duplex.

Kathryn's eyes grew wide and her hand shot to cover her mouth as she looked at Vivienne. "Oh, my."

"Hi?" The teen sounded uncertain.

"The boys were right. You do have a strong resemblance to Alexia and Emma."

Travis's mouth quirked to one side. "Dad's genetics are strong."

Ainsley looked between the blood brothers and had to agree. She would have picked them out of a lineup as being related to each other. They looked more alike than Nathaniel and Noah did. So much for twin DNA.

"You precious child." Kathryn grasped Vivienne's hands then pulled her into a hug. "None of this is your fault. I'm glad we found each other." Her voice did quake a little at those words, though. "The girls will be so thrilled."

"Do you think so?" Vivienne sounded wistful. "They're twins. They have each other and always did. They don't need another sister."

"Oh, I'm not saying it will always be smooth. But yes, I think they'll be delighted."

Ainsley felt relief wash over her at Kathryn's sweet words. Had she expected Nathaniel's gentle mother to be anything but kind and accepting?

She'd been braced for anything, really. Everything could go sideways any minute. The twins didn't know yet. And then there was Declan.

Ainsley's knees quaked at the thought of his blustering anger. She'd tried to prepare her sister, but wasn't that kind of crazy? The man was Vivienne's father. She should hope for wide open arms and acceptance, but that would be more than a miracle.

"Are you staying in Jewel Lake, Vivienne?"

Her sister cast a wide-eyed glance at Ainsley before answering. "I haven't completely decided yet. I only have my Senior year left, and all my friends are in Spokane."

"I did speak with Priscilla on Friday, though," Ainsley said to the group. "If Vivienne wants to enroll in Creekside Academy, she can. Classes aren't too full."

"I heard Mr. Phillips tendered his resignation for high school English the other day. Has Priscilla found a replacement?"

Ainsley couldn't help her widening eyes. "Not yet. Why?"

Kathryn's back seemed to straighten right then and there. "Maybe I'll come to town and talk to her tomorrow."

Oh.

Wow.

CHAPTER TWENTY-TWO

The sound of three teenage girls jabbering and giggling in the backyard as they bonded nearly coaxed a smile to Nathaniel's face, but every time it poked out, he remembered that Declan was due to arrive any minute. If that wasn't enough to sober him and his brothers up, nothing would be.

Mom had retreated to Toby's bedroom with her Bible. Riley and Dakota and Ainsley made small talk in the kitchen. Now that did Nathaniel's heart good, since — if he had his way — Ainsley would soon be one of them.

In the living room, silence reigned. Adam and Noah sat side-by-side on the sofa, each immersed in his own thoughts, while Ryder fidgeted on his phone. Travis paced the space with a near-visible thundercloud hovering above him. Even normally effusive Blake seemed to have no words fit for polite company.

A motor cut out outside, and Riley dragged Dakota through the living room toward the backdoor. "He's here. We'll be praying."

As though anyone had stopped.

It was too late to back out. For a few seconds, Nathaniel fought the urge to flee, but when Ainsley twined her fingers with his, he braced himself. She was done running. He couldn't start.

The door opened, and his stepfather stepped inside. Declan's gaze took in his six sons in no time flat, and his arms crossed over his broad chest as his stance widened. "What's going on here? Where's your mother?"

Nathaniel tugged Ainsley aside as he heard his mom's soft footsteps behind him.

"I'm here, Declan. Come on in, and shut the door."

"I don't think so. This looks like an ambush, and I'm not too fond of that sort of treatment."

Travis reached behind his father and pushed the door shut.

"It kind of is an ambush," Adam said evenly. "We have... concerns we'd like to discuss."

Declan threw his hands to his sides. "Fine. I'll give the Running Creek renters their notice. You can move in. Now, come on, Kathryn."

Considering they'd been pushing Declan to return their dad's ranch to his sons for a year and a half, this should have been cause for rejoicing. At least after they got it in writing. But today's issue was so much bigger, at least for Nathaniel. Maybe even for Adam.

"Thanks." But Adam's single word didn't dissolve the tension.

"What's really going on?" Declan's gaze narrowed on Ainsley's. "Is it still that old, tired thing about your mother and Jason's feeble attempts to fleece Kathryn? You're nothing but a troublemaker, seducing one of my boys for your own agenda."

Nathaniel braced himself, drawing strength from Ainsley's hand tightening in his. "Speaking of seduction for one's own agenda, we know you slept with Ainsley's mother."

Declan rolled his eyes. "Like mother, like daughter. Tramps, both of them."

Nathaniel pushed on. "And we know you knew you're the father of Brenda's other daughter, Vivienne."

"You're grasping at straws." But he gave away his discomfort with his furtive glance at the others in the room.

"I don't think so." Ainsley's voice quivered. "Your name is on Vivienne's birth certificate, and we also know that you sent child support every month." She paused for a beat. "Thank you for that, by the way."

"Faked documents," Declan snarled. "I don't know why you're trying to make me out to be some kind of bad guy, but it's not gonna work. You're all in on this?" He glared at each cowboy in turn as though challenging one to stand by his side. "You, too, Kathryn?"

Mom said nothing, just pursed her lips as she stared back, chin up.

Nathaniel could feel the effort this cost her. She'd been so loyal, taking her marriage vows seriously, far more than Declan deserved. He might not have beaten his wife, but between his temper and his cold shoulder, there were other kinds of abuse. And Nathaniel wouldn't bet his soul on a lack of physical abuse.

Declan's finger pointed at Adam. "Forget what I said.

Long-term renters that give me no lip are gold. The cabin is enough for you and that lying wife of yours."

Adam straightened his shoulders. "I resign from working for Rockstead Ranch, effective immediately. Riley and I will have the cabin vacated by noon tomorrow."

"You can't do that."

"You can't renege on a promise made in front of witnesses and call my wife a liar without receiving the consequences. Yes, Riley and I lied about our relationship. We've come clean and apologized. If you're going to hold old indiscretions against any of us and throw them back in our faces when it suits you, then I can no longer align myself with you."

"Then get off the ranch and don't come back, even to visit your mother."

"That won't be a problem." Mom's voice was thin but strong. "I'm leaving, too."

Red-faced with fury, Declan took three steps toward her, hands fisted at his sides. "You what?"

Nathaniel shifted between them from one side while Noah did the same from the other.

"Hi, Mr. Cavanagh? I'm your other daughter, Vivienne."

They all turned to see Vivienne flanked by the twins.

Declan stared at her, face paling as his mouth opened and closed a few times.

It wasn't often Nathaniel had seen his stepfather at a loss for words.

"Doesn't she look a lot like us, Dad?" asked Alexia. "Don't be a jerk to her. She doesn't deserve it."

Tears hovered on Vivienne's eyelashes and her jaw

trembled. "I've had a hole my entire life that only a father could fill, and now I wish I hadn't found him."

Emma tugged Vivienne into a hug. Alexia joined them.

"See what you've done, Dad?" Travis spoke quietly. "You've got a chance now to make things right. Your actions back then aren't really the issue. You were divorced from Mom and not yet married to Kathryn. Still stupid, but hey, I've been there." He flicked a glance at Nathaniel. "So has Nat. We're not here to judge that."

"Sounds like judgment to me." But some of the bluster had fallen from Declan's voice.

"We'd like to be on your side," Blake said. "All we want is that you acknowledge things and treat us all like human beings that you might even care about. I've seen the evidence that Vivienne's my sister. She seems like a nice kid, and the twins are clearly taken by her. Would it be so terrible to simply say she's your daughter and that you're sorry for the way things went down?"

Declan shook his head. "You sound like a bunch of softies. It's not about emotion. You boys know life is pain and hard work. There's satisfaction in that."

"Emotions are real, too. They're valid. Even Jesus wept." Nathaniel kept his voice level, but it was hard.

"And now we're bringing religion into it."

"Enough, Declan." Mom stepped forward. "You've got a choice to make. You can either keep running roughshod over your entire family, or you can admit that you've made mistakes. The Bible says, 'if we claim to be without sin, we deceive ourselves, and the truth is not in us. But, if we confess our sins, he is faithful and just and will forgive us our sins and purify us from all unrighteousness.'"

"Fancy talk." Some of the bluster had dissipated, though. "I'm not that terrible a man. You've all screwed up, too." His gaze swung between the assembled group. "Now you're so righteous?"

Noah shook his head. "None of us claimed to be perfect. What that verse Mom recited means is that — while we're gonna sin — we just need to admit it and apologize. To God and each other. God's in the forgiving business."

Declan closed his eyes for a couple of seconds and a mask descended over his face. "Kathryn. Twins. It's time to go back to the ranch. Please get in the truck."

"No." Alexia lifted her chin and stared at her father. "Not without our sister."

"No way." Vivienne jerked away from both twins, her eyes filling with tears. "I'm not going anywhere near that man. I wish I'd never heard of him." She dashed out the backdoor.

"Now you've done it, Dad," Emma flung at Declan as she ran after Vivienne, Alexia on her heels.

"Doesn't your Bible say that kids should obey their parents?" Declan snarled at Mom.

She blinked back tears of her own. "It also says fathers should not exasperate their children to wrath. There's a lot about parenting, actually, and I've done a poor job myself."

That seemed to get her husband's attention. "You've been their anchor." He glanced around at their six sons, and he appeared to deflate just a little. "For the boys, too."

"Declan, I've never been one to rock the boat. You know that." Mom closed the space and tugged his hands from behind his back. "But it's time things changed. I wasn't blustering about leaving you. I don't want to, but I can't keep going like this."

"You can't leave me with two teenage girls."

"I won't. They're coming with me."

"Kathryn. Look at me."

Nathaniel wouldn't have believed the softer tone of voice if he hadn't heard it for himself. Half of him wanted to applaud Declan finally showing a bit of emotion, but the other half wanted to warn his mother not to fall for it.

"I'm looking, Declan. You know what I see?"

His eyebrows shot up. "What you see?"

"I see a man too proud to admit he's ever failed. At anything. Ever. A man who must be in control no matter what. It cost you your marriage to Monica—"

"What do you know about that?"

"We've talked a few times."

Declan yanked his hands out of Mom's. "This is ridiculous. What happened to submitting to your husband?"

Way to cherry-pick Bible verses. Seemed the man had latched onto half a dozen that supported his way of thinking.

"Marriage goes both ways, Declan." Adam slid his arm over Mom's shoulders. "Right where it says the bit you seem to know, it also says that men should love their wives as much as Christ loves the church. Which really means to sacrifice everything for their wives."

Declan snorted. "I suppose you're a pro at this. You've been married, what, a year and a half now?"

"I'm no expert, for sure. But I'm willing to admit that and learn from my mistakes." Adam held Declan's gaze. "Are you an expert in marriage?"

Ouch. Way to silence the stepdad.

"I don't need to put up with this from all of you."

"Fancy running Rockstead without the six of us?" Travis drawled. Then he glanced at Noah. "Well, five and a half, since Noah's hardly ever around."

"You wouldn't. The ranch is your life."

"Nope. God is my life. Then Dakota and Toby. I can find another job."

"But…"

"I'm kinda with Trav, here." Blake sounded apologetic. "I don't want to go looking for work, though I hear Sweet River Ranch is hiring. But I'm thinking you and Kathryn need some counseling. Maybe you should get on that."

"You can't mean—"

Counseling? That meant the possibility of Mom and Declan staying together. Nathaniel had been praying for her to leave. Permanently. But maybe his faith had been too weak? Was redemption possible?

Looking at the uncertainty on Declan's face now, maybe it was.

"Blake's onto something," Travis went on. "That's a good prerequisite. You get some counseling. Pastor Marshall could recommend someone, I'm sure. Personal counseling. Counseling for couples."

"Both, I think," Adam put in.

Travis nodded. "And one more thing."

Declan rolled his eyes. "I can't believe this," he muttered.

"We all heard you say you'd give the renters notice so Adam and Riley could move into Running Creek. I expect to be cc'ed on that notification by the end of tomorrow."

"He hasn't earned it," Declan spat out.

"He doesn't have to. He's Joe's son. You'll need to figure out how to deal fairly with Nathaniel and Noah, too."

Declan glared, silenced at least for a few seconds.

"And one more thing." Travis waited a beat. "Dakota and I would like to build a house off the middle section of the ranch drive. That spot where the creek comes near the road. But only if you follow through with the other stuff, because there's no point in moving onto Rockstead if I have to find a job working for some other spread."

"Kathryn."

"Yes?"

Declan jerked his head toward the door. "Are you coming or not?"

"I'm coming."

Instinctively, Nathaniel reached for his mom's arm, but Ainsley held him back.

"I'm coming, but I'm not staying. The boys are right, Declan. We need counseling. We can't keep going like this."

"Like you have anywhere to go."

Mom looked him in the eye as she took his arm and steered him toward the door. "I'm not helpless. Get that through your head."

Nathaniel didn't take another full breath until the truck had pulled away from the duplex.

"Well." Noah dropped dramatically to the sofa. "That went better than I expected."

Adam socked Travis in the shoulder. "Dude. Thanks for sticking up for me."

Travis punched him back. "Cavanagh strong, bro. It's time."

More than time for Running Creek to come back into the family. But seeing the six of them united was worth even more.

"Is your mom serious about leaving my dad?" asked Ryder.

"I think she is. Finally," Nathaniel said slowly.

"Not sure how I feel about that. I mean, I know he's harsh."

Nathaniel glowered at the youngest brother. "And she doesn't deserve harsh. No one does."

"No, I get that, but..." Ryder shook his head. "I need to think about it."

"Is Dad gone?" Emma peeked in the back door.

"He and Mom went up to the ranch." Noah headed toward their sister. "You okay?"

"Mom went with him?" Scowling, Alexia pushed past Emma. "I thought she said she was ditching the loser."

"Respect." Nathaniel's response was automatic.

"He doesn't deserve it!"

"He's still your dad. So, yes, he does deserve it, even though this wasn't his finest day."

Both girls snorted.

"I'll give you a ride up when you're ready to go," put in Ryder. "Blake's got a hot date, or so I hear, and you can't count on any of these other yahoos."

"We're not leaving Vivienne."

"Well, I'm certainly not going to the ranch where I'm clearly not wanted!" came a voice from behind them.

Adam looked from one sister to the other. "Want my opinion?"

"Maybe?" said Emma.

"Probably not," muttered Alexia.

"Go back up the ranch with Ryder when you are ready to go. When Mom figures out what she's doing, it will include you two. She'll take care of you, and we'll all do our part."

"But Vivienne's our sister, too," protested Emma.

"She'll still be right here in Jewel Lake, at least for a few more weeks." Nathaniel wished he could see Vivienne, but she remained outside the door. "Then it's up to her and Ainsley what her plans are for the school year. Things will work out."

His hand chilled when Ainsley let go. She rounded the twins and headed outside to her sister.

Things would work out. Everything was in turmoil right now, but he and Ainsley would come out right-side up. Wouldn't they?

CHAPTER TWENTY-THREE

It had been quite a day. Now Bella was in bed and Vivienne, eyes rimmed in red, had retreated to her room, leaving Ainsley with Nathaniel.

His brows drawn together, Nathaniel studied her. "You okay, honey?"

He was so sweet that she burst into tears. "I don't know. I feel so terrible about everything. It's all my fault."

He set his hands on her shoulders. "What's your fault?"

"Everything. If I hadn't moved here that winter against my mom's wishes, none of this would have happened."

"You mean we wouldn't have met. *Bella* wouldn't have happened."

She sniffled and nodded. "Your whole family has been torn apart."

"Ainsley, love, it's not your fault. None of it is."

"But—"

"Declan already was Vivienne's father. You didn't cause that."

True. She swiped at hot tears.

"Your mom died of cancer. You didn't cause that."

She dared a glance at Nathaniel, but he was right. Again.

"Your mom left you a box that included Vivienne's birth certificate. You would have found that regardless of whether you came to Jewel Lake two and a half years ago. Regardless of whether you and I had ever met."

"I suppose." Ainsley choked out the words.

"My mom and Declan's marriage has been in trouble from the very beginning. That has nothing to do with you, either. This happens to be the thing that gave my mother a backbone and made her decide to leave him, which needed to happen."

"But…"

"Ainsley. The only thing left to regret is Bella and me. Are you sorry about us, too?"

His voice was tender, but the undertow of uncertainty was clear. How could she regret Nathaniel? How could she regret her daughter?

"Nathaniel. I…"

"Ainsley, I love you. I'm sorry — *so* sorry — for not honoring you enough to wait for marriage. But, Bella? She's pretty much perfect. If I could go back in time, knowing what I do now, I'd still choose you. I wouldn't undo Bella, because she's amazing. You're amazing."

Ainsley rubbed at a tender spot on her temple. "You can't mean that."

"I do. Absolutely."

I do. He'd said he'd been set to propose before she'd fled Jewel Lake. She'd have said yes if Declan hadn't threatened her and sent her running. They would have been married by now, and Bella would have known her daddy her entire life.

"Did you hear what Mom said to Declan? About First John chapter one? God forgives us when we ask. He purifies us. Period. Full stop. All we have to do is confess our sin. I've done that. I know you have, too. There's no point in trying to hang onto our guilt, because God has removed it."

Was that what she was doing? Hanging onto her guilt? Maybe. Kind of. The truth was supposed to set her free, but it hadn't worked. Even though everything had been revealed, she still felt trapped.

I am the way and the truth and the life.

Wasn't that what Jesus had said? The truth wasn't about what had happened seventeen years ago. It wasn't about what had happened two years ago, either. The truth was wrapped up in Jesus Himself. No. The truth *was* Jesus. Maybe she needed to reread the context of that verse.

But Nathaniel held her in place, his eyes searching hers, waiting for a response. Oh, she could break away, and he'd let her, but he'd asked a question. Hadn't he? What was it again?

She licked her lips. "Where in the Bible does it talk about the truth setting us free?"

His gaze softened. "We can look it up. I know it's there, but I don't remember exactly." He pulled his phone from his pocket and tapped a few times. "Here it is. John eight, verses thirty-one and thirty-two. 'To the Jews who had believed him, Jesus said, "If you hold to my teaching, you are really my disciples. Then you will know the truth, and the truth will set you free."'"

"If you hold to my teaching," Ainsley breathed. "And Jesus said *He* was the way, the truth, and the life."

Nathaniel nodded slowly, glancing back at his phone. "That's huge."

"I know. I kept thinking that finding out what had really happened — you know, the *truth* — would set me free, but that's not what Jesus meant at all. He meant He is the truth, and He is the one who will set me free." Suddenly unable to hold up her own weight, she dropped down onto the sofa. She'd been looking at that verse all wrong for ages. Declan might be guilty of cherry-picking the few Bible verses he liked, but was she any better?

"Nat, what's going to happen with your mom and Declan?" It wasn't her fault if they split. But she might need to fight the guilt.

He shook his head and settled down beside her. "My truck will be first in line to load her things and move her off the ranch. That job at the academy could be a godsend."

Working with Nathaniel's mom day in and day out would be weird. "And the twins?"

"Maybe it's not too late to enroll them. You mentioned the high school classes aren't full."

And then Vivienne would stay. Wouldn't she? She wanted to get to know her sisters. Wasn't having her stay exactly what Ainsley had hoped for? But sharing would be hard. It had only been the two of them for so long.

Nathaniel slid his arm across her shoulders and tugged her tight. "Don't worry, my love. We've done what we could by exposing the truth." He pressed a kiss to her temple.

The headache that had poked there a minute ago? Gone with his gentle touch.

"Let's leave the rest up to God. He'll do a far better job of working out the details than we could."

Ainsley couldn't quite let go of it yet. "Will you be looking for a new job? Might Declan really fire all of you?"

"Not a chance. He's over a barrel now. The only way he'll save any face at all is giving in. Going to counseling. Working on things with Mom."

She frowned in confusion. "I thought you wanted her to leave."

"I do. But if Declan lets God work in his life, I'd absolutely be in favor of seeing them back together, in time. Sometimes it takes a little space to see what you've had and lost." He nuzzled her hair.

Did he mean what she thought he meant? Or maybe Ainsley was overthinking things again. She glanced toward him.

It seemed he'd been waiting for that. His lips gently teased over hers.

If Nathaniel could set the past aside and love her unconditionally, maybe she could do the same. Ainsley roughed his short hair as she held him close and kissed him back.

CLOUD NINE MAY HAVE HOVERED over Ainsley's townhouse, but there was no evidence of it back at Rockstead Ranch. Nathaniel drove into a silent ranch yard. Sure, it was Sunday evening, but there was always someone around.

One or more of his brothers with the horses. His sisters hanging around. Declan in the office in the stable.

Not today.

Nathaniel wasn't ready to sit in his own small cabin and ponder the day, even if that was what everyone else was apparently doing. He threw a saddle over Kingpin's back and, in a matter of minutes, they trotted up the ranch road.

"Sorry, boy. I've been preoccupied lately." He hadn't ridden much during work hours since they'd been cutting hay on the upper meadows the past couple of weeks, and he'd drawn baler duty. Evenings, he'd been with Ainsley and Bella more often than not.

Kingpin rounded a curve in the wide trail, startling a doe and still-spotted fawn, who leaped into the trees. The hazy smell of warm pines settled over Nathaniel with nary a breeze to waft it away. The only way to get any air movement was to turn Kingpin loose. So he did.

With just a nudge to his ribs, Kingpin burst into full speed, eating the terrain with his long, smooth strides. This gelding could have competed at the Kentucky Derby if he had any bloodlines to speak of, but he was a mutt through and through.

Kingpin exploded over the top of a rise then shied to the right. He would have unseated a less experienced rider, but Nathaniel stayed with him. "Whoa." Not that the word was needed since the gelding had already put on the brakes.

Nathaniel blinked at the sight of his sister sitting on the ground, her horse grazing nearby. "Emma? What's going on?" Also, he should have noticed Desiree's empty stall.

"Hey, Nat." Emma threw aside a handful of dry grass.

He glanced around. "Lex out here, too?"

She shook her head.

Nathaniel swung off Kingpin and dropped the reins to the ground. The gelding sighed, but he'd stay put as long as it was needed. Then Nathaniel lowered himself beside his kid sister. "Talk to me?"

"Are my parents going to get a divorce?" Her voice choked on the word.

The guys might all think the separation was for the best, but that concept seemed not to have reached their sisters. "I don't know," he said at last. "Probably not right away. I think if your dad agrees to talk to Pastor Marshall, they might be able to work things out."

"I don't want them to. I don't want to move to town."

What? Since when? Ah... "Alexia does, right?"

Emma glared at him. "She doesn't think for both of us."

"Hey, I get it. I'm a twin, too. Remember?"

She huffed out a long breath. "Right. Was Noah as pushy as Lex?"

"Sometimes." Nathaniel managed a laugh. "But I thought both of you wanted to go to Creekside Academy with your friends."

"And then come home after school." Emma wiped her arm across her eyes. "I don't want to be a townie."

Maybe she could stay at Rockstead while Alexia went with Mom? But Nathaniel knew better. The girls were even closer than he and Noah had ever been. They only had each other, where he and Noah'd had Adam and then their three stepbrothers.

But... Vivienne. Was this situation part of the problem?

Nathaniel glanced at Emma, where she sat toying with the ends of Desiree's reins.

He should teach her to ground tie her mare.

Maybe not today.

"What do you think of Vivienne?"

Emma shrugged. "She's fine."

"A bit of a surprise, huh?"

"Yeah. My dad's a jerk. But then, you already knew that."

"Respect."

She rolled her eyes. "Seriously, Nat? Can't we be at least a little honest here?"

He draped an arm around his kid sister. "I guess so, as long as we stay polite. But aside from your dad's... mistakes... tell me what you think it will be like having Vivienne as part of your life." His life wouldn't change much. Vivienne would always be Ainsley's sister first in his opinion.

"She and Lex will be best friends, and I'll have no one."

"No way."

"Yes way. It's already started. Putting their heads together and giggling."

"Aw, Em. I'm sorry." He hugged her to his side. He hadn't understood teen girls even when he'd been a teen himself. Ten years hadn't done much to make him an expert. "I think it will even out."

"Really?"

Nathaniel hurt at the hope in her voice. "Yeah, I do. Vivienne will stay living with Ainsley, and—"

"Aren't you going to marry Ainsley?"

"Well, I intend to, but—"

"Vivienne isn't going to live with you then. That would be just gross."

Nathaniel wasn't about to ask why Emma's opinion was so strong. "That's not right away." But why not? It wasn't like he and Ainsley had just met. They'd dated for several months two years ago, and she'd been back in his life six weeks this time around. If he'd been certain of his love back then — and he had been — then what was holding him back now that things were sorted out with Declan?

But Emma brought up a valid point about Vivienne. If she'd gone back to Spokane as originally planned, Ainsley's marriage wouldn't have particularly affected her. Now it sounded like she might stay in Jewel Lake and finish her senior year at the academy. That meant Nathaniel had to think about how marrying her sister affected the teen.

Complicated. Life was much too intricate, even given the fact of how much had been sorted earlier today.

Nathaniel rose to his feet and pulled Emma up. "Kid, you've got six brothers, and we're all on your team. Try not to worry. We've got your back."

She quirked an eyebrow at him. "Team Emma?"

He poked her arm. "Team Twin. Now come on. Race you back to the stable."

"You sure it's going to be okay, Nat?"

He boosted her into the saddle, though she didn't need help. "It will be okay. You know how I know that?"

"Hmm?"

"Because God has a plan. We don't know all the parts of it right now, I'll grant you. That doesn't mean He isn't in control. Yup, things look a mess, but God is way bigger than us. He's got it, Em. He does."

Emma stared at him for a long moment before nodding. Then she pivoted Desiree around and kicked the mare's flanks. "Last one to the stable is a rotten egg."

Nathaniel grinned and shook his head. He ambled over to Kingpin and swung to his back. "Let's go, boy. We'll show her who's got it."

CHAPTER TWENTY-FOUR

Nathaniel wouldn't have been certain his stepfather even returned for the night if a few things in Diesel's box pen hadn't been moved a few inches.

Mom was resolute. She'd spoken with Priscilla Cantrell on Monday morning and been gladly offered the high school teaching job. It helped that she'd taught at the academy years before and kept current since with just enough online classes to retain her accreditation.

Dakota had rounded up a two-bedroom apartment for Mom and the twins not far from Ainsley's place. The girls were in their rooms packing and arguing over the small space they'd be sharing.

Nathaniel was just as glad to be two floors down in Mom's garden suite, helping Adam load boxes Dakota had scored behind retail stores in town yesterday.

He hefted a small, sturdy box. "What's in here, Mom?"

His mother swept a few loose strands of hair behind her ear. "A few mementoes from my grandmother."

"Like what? Have we ever seen them displayed?" asked Adam.

"At Running Creek." Mom eyed the box. "Pass me that utility blade, and I'll show you. Then you'll remember."

Nathaniel shook his head. "We don't have to do that now."

"I'd like to see them myself." Mom cut the tape, opened the flaps, and moved aside some shredded paper. "My grandmother made tea parties for my sister and me with these cups and saucers." She held up a dainty floral pattern then set it on the table. "I broke the creamer when I was little. I cried and cried because something so beautiful and fragile had been lost forever. But, I was wrong."

She held up a little pitcher that had obviously been fractured then repaired with what looked like gold.

Nathaniel's brows furrowed as he held out his palm, and Mom set the piece in it. "This looks amazing. What happened?"

"My grandfather had a Japanese friend who'd been trained in the art of kintsugi. In this tradition, the damage done to a piece of china or pottery is repaired with lacquer and gold to draw attention to the flaws and beautify them. It always reminds me of my favorite verse in Isaiah. God sent the prophet to 'comfort all who mourn, and provide for those who grieve in Zion — to bestow on them a crown of beauty instead of ashes, the oil of joy instead of mourning, and a garment of praise instead of a spirit of despair.'"

Her finger lightly traced one of the gold lines. "Thanks for asking what was in this box, Nat. I'd forgotten about this little pitcher. At the time, it helped make a little girl feel better about having broken a precious object, but right now — today — it means so much more. I think this is going to go in a place of honor in the apartment. I need to recall its lesson."

"That pattern…" Nathaniel said slowly. "It seems familiar."

"It was fairly popular when I was young, so you might have seen it in other people's houses."

Adam poked him. "Or you might remember it from when you were a kid, because we don't really hang out in the *fine china* crowd."

Nathaniel shook his head. "I know where. Ainsley has a sugar bowl just like this. It was from her grandmother."

"Like I said, quite common in that era. People put more stock in crystal and china and real silver pieces back then."

He tucked the pitcher back in its nest of shredded paper. "I'd like to show it to Ainsley when you unpack it in town."

"Sure."

Adam ran packing tape down the box, sealing the contents once more. He carried it out to the waiting truck.

"Are you going to propose to her soon?"

"Yeah, I am. I'm waiting for the dust from all the rest of this to settle a bit first." He winced as he thought of how that might sound to his mother.

"Don't wait too long."

Nathaniel studied his mom's sad face. "Do you still believe in love? In marriage?"

Her gaze flew to meet his. "I absolutely do. I have faith that things will work out with Declan. I've never seen him so… humbled."

Nathaniel wasn't sure that was the right word, but he'd

let it go. "We'll definitely be praying for you two. And for the girls."

Mom sighed. "I wish I knew if I was doing the right thing for them."

"You are," Adam said firmly as he came back in. "Things couldn't keep going the way they were. It wasn't healthy for anyone."

"Part of me feels a bit better now that I've made a decision, but part of me is panicking that I jumped too suddenly."

"Seventeen years isn't exactly sudden." Adam tugged Mom against his side. "All six of us will be praying for you and helping out with the twins however we can. You're not alone."

Not alone.

There had been plenty of times Nathaniel resented the press of brothers around him, but still, he wouldn't trade the lot of them for anything.

Except maybe for Ainsley.

"Hi, love." Nathaniel kissed Ainsley when he came in the door.

She'd missed him all day, even while she'd been at work, and she knew he'd been helping his mom and sisters move. Now she just wanted to melt into his embrace, but he kept one hand behind his back. "What've you got there?" Maybe flowers.

He offered a quick grin then he glanced around the room, his gaze finally landing on the pantry cart she'd picked up to supplement the kitchen's meager storage. He caught her hand and pulled her toward it.

What on earth?

"Ah, just as I thought." Nathaniel reached out, reverently touching the little sugar bowl from her grandmother with the broken arms inside of it.

"As you thought?" Ainsley repeated.

But then he set a matching cream pitcher beside it and stepped back.

Matching... except where the creamer had been repaired with... gold? Ainsley leaned closer. "Where did you get that?"

"It's my mom's, from her own grandmother. She broke it when she was little, and her grandfather had it repaired by a Japanese craftsman he knew. Isn't that cool?"

She looked between the two pieces: one broken, one restored. "It's amazing. It's... almost better than it was."

Nathaniel wrapped both arms around her from behind and kissed the side of her neck. "Not almost. It really is better. Before, it was just a regular little pitcher. Now it's a work of art."

Ainsley blinked back a few tears. "It's a testament to God using broken people."

"That's what I wanted you to see in it. You and I — we made some big mistakes a couple of years ago. I'm sorry, but I'm not going to keep apologizing, because now I can see that God has totally used that to bring about something even more beautiful than it could have been otherwise."

"You're talking about Bella."

"I am." He nuzzled her neck. "But not only her. We are

where we are today because of those broken pieces and how God has restored them. The whole package."

Ainsley turned in Nathaniel's embrace and looped her arms around his neck. "I love you, Nathaniel Cavanagh."

"I love you, too, Ainsley Johnson." His lips brushed hers.

"Whoops. Excuse me."

Ainsley smiled against Nathaniel's mouth at Vivienne's words and leaned back a little to glance at her sister. "Look what Nathaniel brought over."

Vivienne touched the little creamer. "That's cool. Can we do the same thing with the sugar bowl?"

"With your permission, I want to try. I'm no Japanese craftsman, but there are YouTube tutorials that make it look very possible."

Moisture flooded Ainsley's eyes. "You'd do that for me?"

"Oh, baby. There isn't much I wouldn't do for you." His voice grew husky.

"Outta here!" called Vivienne as her footsteps pounded up the stairs. Hopefully, she wouldn't disturb Bella.

Warm wrinkles appeared around Nathaniel's eyes as he smiled at Ainsley. "Maybe now things will settle down a little. Vivienne's staying, I hear?"

"Yes. She wants to get to know her sisters."

"You've got concerns?"

Ainsley let out a shaky laugh. "It sounds silly, but I'm not used to sharing her. We've always just had each other, so this will be a big change."

"It's a big change for the twins, too. Emma's worried she'll be the one left out."

"Oh, no! I didn't even think of it that way, like Viv would be breaking their bond."

"She won't. They're all growing up. There are adjustments every which way, but don't you know? Love only gets stronger if it's shared."

"I don't like sharing." She pressed a quick kiss to his lips. "I want you all to myself."

Nathaniel chuckled. "That's not exactly what I meant. I want you all to myself, too." He studied her.

"But there's Bella."

"Different again. She's both of ours."

If it hadn't been their daughter he was thinking of, what had caused that thoughtful look?

"Sweetheart, are we ready?" he asked softly.

Ready? For — oh! "It depends?"

"Two years ago, I had a big production planned, which I guess was kind of silly since we're both such private people. But lots of things have happened in the interim. They've become like the gold veins decorating that little pitcher and holding it together. Ainsley…" He caressed her shoulders as he searched her face. "I love you so much, and I want to spend the rest of my life proving it to you. Will you marry me?"

Ainsley cradled his dear face between her palms and looked intently into his eyes. "I'd like nothing better, Nathaniel. I love you, and Bella loves you."

He dug into his pocket and pulled out a small box. "I've had this for two years," he admitted. "I never lost hope I'd find you again, that I'd get the chance to give this to you." He tipped the lid open. "I'm sorry for jumping the gun that day at the park."

The brilliant princess-cut diamond gleamed from its white-gold setting. She couldn't help the soft gasp coming from her mouth. "Nat, it's beautiful." She hadn't really gotten a good look at it before.

"Not half as beautiful as you, my love. Will you wear it?"

"I'd be honored." After all those months of not remembering, of believing her mother's lies about the man who'd fathered Ainsley's baby, of debilitating headaches... after all those months of certainty she'd be a single mom forever, Nathaniel's love and forgiveness was a gift greater than she could fathom.

He slipped the ring onto her finger, the perfect size. How had he known? It didn't matter.

Questions danced in her mind. When could they plan a wedding? Where would they live? Would Nathaniel even keep working for his stepfather at Rockstead Ranch? Would Declan and Kathryn's marriage be redeemed? Would the three teen girls sort out their relationships?

But the flurry settled when Nathaniel's mouth claimed hers. They'd work everything out later. There was plenty of time.

Their future was sealed. Together.

EPILOGUE

Another one bites the dust.

Blake Cavanagh helped himself to a hamburger in his brother Travis's backyard while keeping an eye on his dad standing awkwardly beside the fence. The whole clan had come together to celebrate Nathaniel and Ainsley's engagement, and this might be the first time his dad and Kathryn had been in the same place at the same time since they'd split up a few weeks ago.

Dad had tried to get out of coming, but Travis had refused to put up with his nonsense. Cavanagh strong and all that. Sure, Dad had adopted the Anderson boys and given them his surname all those years ago, but the family was fractured now. As far as Blake was concerned, his step-brothers could take their own father's name back again, claim their hobby-sized ranch, and get out of Rockstead.

Or not. He didn't much care. Rockstead was big enough for them all.

It definitely wasn't worth a big battle to keep this crew

together with their parents separated. Divorces happened all the time. The couples split their assets, dealt with the consequences, and got on with their lives.

"Whaddya think?" Ryder stood beside him, holding out a bowl of potato chips.

"Think? About what?"

"Whatever's got you scowling like a bull pawing the dirt."

"Am not." Blake helped himself to a handful of chips and tossed some back.

"Are, too." Ryder laughed then looked around. "Am I the only one who thinks this party is just a little awkward?"

"You may still be wet behind the ears, but you figured this one out. It *is* awkward."

"I'm not that young." Ryder rolled his eyes then beckoned around the group. "So, you gonna be next?"

"Next to get hitched? I doubt it."

"Did Felicity and Arlene ever figure out you were two-timing them?"

"I haven't tried to keep it a secret. Plus, I took Marnie out last week."

"You're nuts."

"I told you. I'm not ready to get serious." Blake eyed his kid brother. "And you're too young to settle down. You're four years younger than me."

"I didn't realize we had to queue up by age."

"It's an unspoken rule." Blake smacked Ryder's shoulder. "Why, are you dating someone?"

"Like I'd tell you if I was."

Now that was funny. They worked together day in, day

out at the ranch. Nobody's secrets lasted long. Even Nathaniel's hadn't.

Blake glanced over at the newly engaged couple. Nathaniel's face practically glowed when he looked at Ainsley.

But then, the Anderson boys had a different legacy than the born-and-bred Cavanaghs. Their dad had loved their mother wholeheartedly, while Blake's father had bulldozed his way through two marriages. Blake wouldn't blame Kathryn if she closed the door on reconciliation. It would serve his pigheaded father right.

He wasn't going to be like his dad, but he didn't have the same genetics as the Andersons, either. Actually falling in love was too risky. He'd wind up hurting the unlucky woman and thus himself in the process.

No, thanks. He'd be better off alone.

A NOTE FROM VALERIE:

Oh, Blake. I can't blame you for trying to guard your heart. Your family history has really messed you up, and you're struggling to believe God has a 'best plan' for your life that you can gladly embrace. Set the past aside, Blake. Reach for the future in *Kiss Me Like You Mean It, Cowboy*.

Dear Reader, did you miss Adam and Riley's love story or Travis and Dakota's? You'll find all the Cavanagh Cowboys Romances at valeriecomer.com/cavanagh.

ACKNOWLEDGMENTS

Ah, cowboys! There's just something about them, isn't there? Masculine, hardworking, resourceful, honorable, and gentlemanly... a cowboy is hard to beat.

Thank YOU, dear reader, for loving the Saddle Springs Romance series so much I was inspired to write the Cavanagh Cowboys Romance series as a spin-off. I hope you enjoy the ride. Pun intended!

Always, always, thanks to my fellow author and friend, Elizabeth Maddrey. She prods, cheers, and commiserates as needed, then offers helpful brainstorming and critiques. If you haven't read her Christian contemporary romances, go find them and get started!

My amazing editor, Nicole, has been with me from the beginning. She went above and beyond the call of duty this time, going through the manuscript not once, not twice, but three times before she felt I'd 'nailed it.' I am so thankful for her!

I'm also grateful for the Christian Indie Authors Facebook group and my sister bloggers at Inspy Romance.

These folks make a difference in my life every single day. I'm thrilled to walk beside them as we tell stories for Jesus!

Thank you to my Facebook friends, followers, street team, and reader group members for prayers, encouragement, and great fellowship. If you'd like to join other readers who love my stories, please find us at Valerie Comer: Readers Group.

Thanks to my husband, Jim, whose love for me never fails and who encourages me in every endeavor. Thanks to my kids, their spouses, and my wonderful grandgirls for cheering me on. To them, having an author for a mom/grandma is "normal." Imagine that!

All my love and gratitude goes to Jesus, the One who is my vision, the High King of Heaven, the lord of my heart. Thank you. A thousand times, thank you.

ABOUT VALERIE COMER

Valerie Comer's life on a small farm in western Canada provides the seed for stories of contemporary Christian romance. Like many of her characters, Valerie grows much of her own food and is active in the local foods movement as well as her church. She only hopes her imaginary friends enjoy their happily-ever-afters as much as she does hers, shared with her husband, adult kids, and adorable grand-daughters.

Valerie is a *USA Today* bestselling author and a two-time Word Award winner. She writes engaging characters, strong communities, and deep faith into her green clean romances.

To find out more, visit her website at www.valeriecomer.com, where you can read her blog, explore her many links, and sign up for her email newsletter, where you will find news, giveaways, deals, book recommendations and more. You can also find Valerie blogging with other authors of Christian contemporary romance at Inspy Romance.